The Alien Transcripts

~

Creating God

James Kelly

ISBN: 1-886726-32-9

ISBN-13: 978-1-886726-32-1

Library of Congress Control Number: 2018952280

SAN: 256-5846

www.mammothstarpublishing.com

www.authorjameskelly.com

www.aspectsofwriting.com

The Alien Transcripts

MAMMOTH STAR PUBLISHING
5244 SUNNY BEACH LANE
LAS VEGAS, NV 89118

COVER CONCEPT BY JAMES KELLY
COVER DESIGN BY JAMES KELLY and JOHN LONG
COVER GRAPHICS BY JIM ROBBINS and JAMES KELLY

CONTENTS

INTRODUCTION

Based on the original book, *Creating God*, *The Alien Transcripts* has been revised in order to make the premise of the story more plausible.

The idea for this book originated in 1990 from my viewing of a documentary, which discussed the consequences of man depleting the rainforests of the world and the effect that man has on the extinction of primates and other species.

As the camera switched between the primates and their remaining habitats, and the surrounding towns and cities that now occupy segments of the rainforest where they once roamed, I noticed a resemblance between those primates and man. I observed similarities in their mannerisms and in their facial and physical structure. This varied with each region of the world that the filmmaker visited.

Although certain I am not the first person to have made such observations, this revelation was the beginning of my adventure, of my awareness of the probability that man did evolve. The relevance of that documentary was the beginning of the notion that perhaps the evolution of current man is due to a possible intervention - and so the story begins.

CHAPTER 1
The Abduction

SUNDAY - 8:35 p.m.

Dusk falls over the Mojave Desert. The springtime air has chilled from a light breeze that stirs from high up in the mountains, and the smell of a light rain, from an isolated and unpredicted thundercloud, now far off in the distance, permeates the usually dry and dusty surroundings. A family of four has perched themselves on top of an overlook just a few miles outside of Jean, Nevada. The stars and moon illuminate the night sky, creating an iridescent glow over the otherwise bone-dry riverbed below. In the desolate landscape of the valley, cactus and tumbleweed populate the rocky terrain. An occasional mound protrudes from the sandy sediment that is as old as the Earth itself.

The father helps his twelve-year-old daughter set up the telescope she received for her birthday, while the mother and younger brother observe the stars with binoculars. Once the scope is in place, the father focuses in on what appears to be a comet streaking across the sky in their direction.

Noticing the light, the daughter whines, tugging at his jacket. "Come on, Dad, let me see. It's my telescope."

The mother chides her husband. "Let her look while you set up your own, Dear."

"Okay, Okay."

The father relinquishes the telescope and picks up his own tripod, while the daughter hurries to view the object.

Glancing over at his daughter as he sets up his tripod, her father offers a suggestion. "If you position the lens toward the constellation Corona Borealis, you'll be able to see the comet."

"I know what to do, Dad. I can see it."

"Okay, okay. Gees." His attention turns back to setting up his equipment.

Momentarily, all are silent as his daughter alters the lens on her telescope.

Suddenly, she cries out, "Dad, come here, Hurry!"

Her brother rushes up to sneak a peek, but she pushes him away.

Having secured his telescope, her father becomes curious and pivots to see why she is so excited. "What? What is it?"

She continues to adjust the lens, focusing in on the phenomenon as it draws nearer. However, the object is moving so fast toward them that it is hard to follow. Her mother and brother have a difficult time viewing the streaking mass with their binoculars.

Confused about what she sees, she tries to describe it, stammering, "There's something really weird ... I mean ... I don't know ... it looks ... it looks like a ..."

Before she finds the words to characterize her observation, a solid dark and massive object passes overhead. It generates a strong gust of wind that knocks them and their telescopes to the ground.

"Daddy, what was that?" The girl is scared as she scurries to set the telescope back into position.

So as not to further frighten the children, her mother replies, "It was probably just a dust devil."

"That was no dust devil, Mom." The daughter states without hesitation, and then turns her telescope in the direction of the objects last sighting.

Her father, mother, and brother watch in the same direction with one hand above their eyes to block out the moonlight. They witness something bright flicker from behind a mound, out on the desert floor below. With the scope reset, the daughter hurries to focus in on the glow.

She shouts, "I don't believe it!"

"Believe what?" Her brother tries to push her out of the way, so that he can see.

Disregarding his attempt, she returns to a blurry image in the sight of her telescope, and focuses the lens. The silhouette of what appears to be a face develops. After final adjustment, a clear image of an oblong face with huge eyes, a small mouth, and perfectly smooth skin emerges. It becomes apparent by its stare that this being has centered in on her.

Frenzied, the girl exclaims, "Quick Daddy! Come look. Hurry."

Her father rushes at the sound of the urgency in her voice and gazes into the lens. He views a glimpse of the face, then the light behind the mound disappears, and darkness closes in around the lens of the telescope.

"Do you see it, Dad? Do you see it?" His daughter is full of hopeful excitement.

He is apprehensive about what he witnessed. "No, Sweetheart, I didn't. I didn't see anything."

"But, Dad, you must have seen it!" she shouts. "You had to have. It was an alien!"

As frustration takes over, a tear flows down her cheek. "I swear, Dad, it was an alien."

He draws his daughter near in an effort to comfort her. "I believe you, sweetheart. I believe you."

MONDAY - 6:15 a.m.

Out on the desert, the family examines the base of the mound where they witnessed the bizarre event of the night before.

In the distance, a car passes by on the lonesome highway. The driver, Daniel, a tall, slim man, observes the family through his driver's side window. Exploring the Mojave Desert is a common pastime for folks, so without giving it any thought,

Daniel passes without hesitation.

Half an hour later Daniel arrives at a private airstrip in Las Vegas. He parks his car and boards a twin-engine plane bound for Area 51. The plane lands at the top-secret government installation twenty-five minutes later. Agent Daniel Scudder, an intense person in his early forties with a light complexion and hazel eyes, exits the plane. He approaches Chief Willian Rankin, who is the head of the Terrestrials Project for the FBI. The two men climb into a nearby golf-cart, and drive to a facility located within the Area 51 compound. The chief briefs Daniel about a new case as they drive toward the facility.

LATER THAT NIGHT

Daniel proceeds up the hall from his office to that of Special Agent Mary Drake, his partner for the Terrestrials Project. In her late thirties, Mary is a physically fit woman, short in stature, meticulously groomed, with long, wavy, auburn hair. A member of the American Society of Clinical Hypnosis, Mary studied hypnotherapy while obtaining a PsyD in Psychology at Harvard University. It is her responsibility to place reported victims of abduction under hypnosis to ascertain the validity of their stories.

Daniel opens the door to Mary's office and finds Mary sitting at her desk, transcribing notes from a recorder into her computer.

"Hey, Agent Drake, I'm heading out."

"Okay. And, Daniel, you can drop the formalities. We're the only two people here. I'll see you in the morning. I would like to wrap up the Milliner case before I leave this evening."

"I can stay if you want?" Daniel holds up a gristle-like object the size of a shot pellet in a small, clear evidence bag. "I need to drop this specimen off to be analyzed, and then I can stop back by before taking the shuttle home."

"No, no, you go on. I'll take a later shuttle. Oh, and depending on how late I am, I may sleep in tomorrow morning. No need to pick me up."

Concerned, Daniel questions, "That's two days in a row. Honey, are you mad at me?"

"What? Don't be silly, Daniel. I would just like to wrap this case up. I'm tired of dealing with it. I swear, these cases get more outrageous every day." Mary stops typing and looks over at Daniel. "Uh, oh, I forgot. That thing you're holding between your fingers is from the Milliner case, isn't it?"

Daniel ignores her sarcastic remark. "That's okay, Babe, you continue to play the Doubting Thomas, and I'll continue to play the believer. Although, I must admit, after nearly fourteen years of chasing extraterrestrials, I'm beginning to have my own doubts they exist."

"Now that I find bizarre."

"Well, the truth is," Daniel says, holding up the bag and examining it, "out of the hundreds of cases we've studied, we still haven't been able to come up with one concrete piece of evidence that aliens are among us." He devilishly mocks her earlier comment. "Uh, oh, what's this? I believe it's the implant removed from Mr. Milliner's nostril. And, wouldn't you know it? It was right where he said the aliens placed while on board their ship. The same, I might add, as a few of the other abductees you questioned under hypnosis."

Mary quips, "Do I detect a bit of sarcasm?"

"What, me sarcastic?" He becomes serious for a moment. "You know, it could be an implant. I am trained to keep an open mind, remember?"

Mary giggles.

"Why are you giggling? It really could be an implant."

"I'm not laughing at that, silly, I'm laughing at you and me. How long have I known you?"

Confused at her question, Daniel adds a little more sarcasm back into his response. "Well, we were brought together on this project about fourteen years ago, so I guess the answer would have to be … about fourteen years?"

"And for twelve of those fourteen, you barely acknowledged my existence."

"I'm thinking, not true. Of course I've acknowledged you."

Mary points out the obvious. "As a colleague, yes, but as a woman, no."

"You just said it, you were a colleague. So, what was I supposed to do?"

"I don't know. What did you do two years ago to

get my attention that was different from the prior twelve?"

Daniel thinks for a moment. "I'm confused, what the hell are we talking about? What does all of this have to do with the implant?"

"First of all, Daniel, you know it is highly improbable that what you are holding in your hand is an implant. My point is this. It took you twelve years to notice me. I'm talking about outside the job, the real me, the person you've come to know. I did everything but rape you to get your attention. Yet, you acted as though I didn't even exist."

"Mary, we work together every day. Therefore, it goes without saying you exist."

"So, why did it take you so long to come around? I'm right here with you practically every day. Yet, you want to believe in something that has no tangible probability of existence."

"Honey, listen to yourself. You're talking about apples and oranges."

Mary half-heartedly agrees. "Okay, let's take me out of the equation. I still don't understand how you can continue to believe in something that has shown no inkling of being real for all of these years?"

"Ah, maybe because it's my job? And I would have to disagree." He holds up the object again.

Mary ignores him. "Actually, it's your job to investigate reported abductions, just as it's my job to analyze the abductees through hypnosis. All I know is that in all of my years of analyzing the self-proclaimed abducted, my conclusions have always been the same. I still haven't heard or seen one ounce of evidence that extraterrestrials exist. What I do hear is the same story repeatedly, a story created, and then hyped, by the media. I'm beginning to wonder why our government continues with this program."

"Oh, and, besides, I did notice you. I just didn't acknowledge your existence beyond work. Big difference."

Mary pauses and then smirks at him.

Daniel glances down at his watch. "Okay, Babe, I've got to go. I need to get this sample over to the Area 52 lab before Tommy leaves. Besides, I'm holding you up from finishing your report. I'll see you in the morning."

"That's fine. We can finish debating this over dinner tomorrow night."

"Your place, or mine?"

"Check your calendar. We're supposed to have dinner tomorrow with my mother and father. Remember? It's their 50th wedding anniversary." Mary realizes from the expression on his face he has forgotten.

"I'm glad that you reminded me. Lord knows that if I didn't show up, you would think that I had done it on purpose. And since we're on the subject of anniversaries, I'd like you to make me a promise."

"What's that?"

"Promise me on our 50th, you won't invite one of our kids, or aliens, to tag along. It's our anniversary, not theirs." Daniel grins.

"Isn't that a bit premature, since we aren't even engaged? Wait, Daniel, is that a proposal?"

"We'll talk about it tomorrow, after dinner," Daniel turns to leave, then stops. "Oh, and one more thing - I love you."

Having only spoken those words once before, Mary looks at him and declares with heartfelt astonishment, "I love you too."

Daniel closes the door behind him. A short distance down the hallway, he exits the building and reaches a company car. He opens the car door, and then stops briefly to gaze at the stars, as though something beckons him. After the feeling passes, he gets in his car and drives off in the direction of the Area 52 compound, located in the foothills adjacent to Area 51.

Driving down the dark and desolate stretch of road between compounds, Daniel is compelled to look again at the star-filled sky. From out of nowhere, a bright light appears above the car. The gages, radio, and lights on the car flicker off and on. While trying to maintain control, he watches the object as it hovers overhead. Then, in an instant, the light vanishes.

A little frightened, and uncertain of what transpired, Daniel glances in his rearview mirror. For a brief moment, the light reappears, then disappears, just as rapidly. As he continues to drive, Daniel ponders what he may have encountered.

AREA 52 - 8:30 p.m.

Daniel arrives at the security gate and shows his credentials to the guard. He is permitted entry and the gate opens. He drives to one of the labs within the compound, parks the car, and approaches the entrance to the building. After entering a code, a laser scans his eyes, and he opens the door. Daniel enters the lab and finds Tommy, a scientist for the Terrestrials Project.

Tommy is a man in his early thirties, of medium build, and Indian descent. He hears the door open and swivels around from his microscope.

Daniel approaches Tommy with the gristle-like material in his hand. "Well, Tommy, my friend, this is the specimen that we retrieved from Mr. Milliner's nose. It's ready for your expert inspection."

He hands Tommy the container.

"Another one, huh? I'm sure I'll come to the same conclusion as with the others." Tommy holds the plastic bag containing the specimen up to the ceiling light to examine it before placing it on the table. "Let's see what it looks like under the scope." He removes the specimen from the bag and places it under the microscope's lens.

"I thought you said you were unable to determine the composite structure of the last device?"

While inspecting the gristle-like material through the scope, Tommy chuckles. "I wouldn't call it a device. I'm sorry if I led you to believe that the other specimens you brought to me were anything other than earthly. I'm sure you are aware that when the human body ingests a foreign substance it is able to break it down and modify it into unidentifiable compounds. If not for your discovery, the substance would otherwise be unknown to man. The human body is perhaps man's greatest mystery. As scientists, we are still unable to determine all it is capable of."

"So you believe that these specimens were formed inside the human body?" Daniel inquires.

"Well I still need to conduct a few chemical tests on the specimen. What I'm suggesting is that we don't get carried away. Thus far, I'm absolutely certain the genetic make-up of all the specimens I have examined is similar to silicone. It is my summation that with all of the additives placed in our foods, the body has found a way to break down those compounds, or toxins, and store them like it does cellulite or fat."

Daniel is unconvinced. "How do you explain its perfect shape?"

"How do you explain the perfect shape of our teeth or our eyes? I realize that our job is to determine if aliens exist ..." Tommy looks up from the microscope to Daniel, "... but before I can announce we have something from outer space in our possession, I need to prove conclusively, that this is a substance completely unknown to man." He turns back to the scope. "To date, I'm not convinced that this specimen, like all the others that have been presented to me, is anything other than a physical reaction to a foreign compound ingested by the human body."

Somewhat disheartened, Daniel makes a concession. "Well, you are the expert. After all, I can't argue with science now, can I?"

Tommy pats his colleague on the back. "I know how you must feel. However, I'm a scientist, and unless I'm shown beyond any doubt that this is a compound unknown to man, I have to maintain that it is not alien in origin. Quite simply, I deal in reality based on facts."

"You're right." Daniel reluctantly agrees as he glances at his watch. "Listen, it's getting late. Get back to me if you discover something out of the ordinary."

"Don't worry, Danny my friend, you'll be the first to know."

"Thanks. See you Later."

After exiting the building, he drives to the main gate, where the guard recognizes him and waves him through.

Assured that Daniel is gone, Tommy makes a phone call. He dials, and then listens for a voice to answer on the other end.

Once the phone is answered, Tommy responds, "This is Agent Orr ... Yes, sir, I have the device in my hand as we speak ... No, sir, he doesn't suspect a thing. I'm positive."

TWO HOURS LATER

While driving from the Las Vegas airstrip toward home, Daniel gazes up at the stars and begins talking to himself. "If you're out there, what's the big secret? What could you possibly gain from sitting back and watching? Maybe, Mary is right. Maybe, we've both wasted fourteen years of our lives chasing the improbable."

CHAPTER 2
The Revelation

AREA 51 – Wednesday - 8:00 a.m.

Daniel nurses a nosebleed with a tissue as he casually strolls down the hall. He acknowledges a couple of colleagues and Chief Rankin. The chief notices Daniel as he passes, and walks out of his office. He quickens his pace as he follows Daniel. Oblivious to the chief's presence, Daniel enters his office with Chief Rankin at his heels. Daniel walks around the side of his desk and sits. As he scoots his chair in toward the desk, and raises his head, Daniel, who is already in a skittish mood, becomes startled by the chief's sudden appearance.

"Oh! Chief ... good morning, Sir."

Chief Rankin, now standing in front of the desk with his arms crossed notices that Daniel's skin is bright red. It appears to be a bad sunburn. A trickle of blood drips from Daniel's nose, and he dabs it with a blood soaked tissue.

"What's up with the nose, Agent Scudder?"

"Nothing, Sir. It's just a nosebleed."

Daniel looks at the bloodstained tissue, tosses it into the trashcan beside his desk, and reaches for another one. Chief Rankin, without saying a word, stretches his arms and places his hands on the edge of the desk, as if waiting for Daniel to say something.

"I'm sorry, Chief, did you need something?"

"Where in the hell have you been, Scudder?"

Daniel reasons that perhaps he is late because his wristwatch has stopped. He glances down at his watch and notices the second hand is still moving. Therefore, he determines there must be a different reason for what seems to be an off-the-wall question.

Daniel is confused. "I'm not sure what you mean, sir? I'm on time, according to my watch."

Chief Rankin scolds Daniel. "You know to what I'm referring."

Puzzled, Daniel responds, "I do?"

The chief explains himself. "I got a call yesterday from the top brass. He wanted to know where we were with the Milliner case."

"Chief, I informed you yesterday of our progress, remember? I told you that I was taking the sample removed from Mr. Milliner's nostril over to the Area 52 lab to be analyzed."

"Scudder, you weren't here yesterday. Too much sun affecting your memory?"

"Chief, I was here all day. Remember, we talked about the similarities between the Milliner case and the Larson's daughter."

"That was Monday."

"Correct, sir. And this is Tuesday."

"No, Scudder, this is Wednesday. Stop playing games. If you wanted an extra day off, all you had to do was ask. Lord knows you deserve a vacation, but put in for it. Are you aware that I put out an APB on you?"

"What?"

"That's right. No one could reach you, and Drake got worried. Agent Sykes was in Vegas, so I sent him over to your place to see if you were okay. Since your car was missing, and there was no sign of foul play, we concluded you must have had an accident. After checking with the police, the hospitals, and the morgue, collectively, we ruled that out. The notion of a kidnapping entered the picture, that is, until Drake divulged you were supposed to have dinner with her parents last night. I can understand trying to avoid your girlfriend's parents, but that is not an excuse for failing to show up for work."

"Chief, this can't be Wednesday. I get it. This is a joke, right?"

"Look, Scudder, we all deserve an extra day off once in a while. I'm not faulting you for whatever you did yesterday, but when the head of the bureau calls and wants to know where one of his top agents is and I can't tell him because I don't know ..."

"Chief, I swear, I don't have a clue as to what the hell you're talking about."

"Scudder, you've been with this agency for what, thirteen, fourteen years, and to my knowledge you've never pulled a stunt like this before. I am willing to overlook your silly charade, this time. I don't give a damn where you were yesterday. However, the next time, and there had better not be a next time, I'm not sure that I'll be able to excuse this type of behavior so readily. At the very least, you could have left a message on your voice mail stating your whereabouts."

"But, Chief ..."

"End of discussion. We have a briefing at 1400 hours. You are expected to be there."

"Yes, Sir."

Chief Rankin storms out of the office, leaving Daniel perplexed. Dumbfounded, Daniel fidgets at his desk as he tries to understand what happened. He notices his hands have a red hue but is more concerned about the conversation with the chief. He checks the date on his watch, then at his desk calendar. Uncertain whether he is being spoofed, or if Chief Rankin is serious, Daniel picks up the phone and pushes a button on the handset. A woman answers on the other end.

"Katie, my favorite receptionist, this is Agent Scudder."

"I'm your only receptionist."

"Right. Anyway, I have a question for you. What is today's date?"

"Is this a trick question?"

"No, no, this is not a trick question."

"Wednesday, May 17th."

"Okay, thank you."

Daniel hangs up the phone and is more perplexed than ever. He stands and pauses in thought, then enters the hall and proceeds to Mary's office. He knocks on the door.

"Come in, it's open," Mary says from inside.

Daniel timidly opens the door and enters. Mary's back is to him as he walks in and stands beside her desk. She looks up from her computer. Realizing it is Daniel, she ignores him and returns to her typing.

Daniel is bewildered by her reaction. "Mary, please tell me that I'm not going insane."

She does not react.

He prods her further. "Are you okay?"

Mary ignores him and continues with her work.

Daniel wonders if she is a participant in some kind of prank. "Come on, Mary, not you too?"

She pretends he is not there.

"Mary, please! What in Sam Hill is going on around here?"

She looks up from the keyboard with cold eyes and glares at him. Mary notices the red hue and thinks he was sunning on the day before. "I don't know, Daniel, why don't you tell me?"

"This is crazy." Daniel shakes his head.

"Crazy! I'll give you crazy. Crazy is my believing in you! What was the point of our conversation on Monday night? Obviously, not much. How insensitive can a person be? You could at least have called if you didn't want to go to dinner with my parents."

Befuddled as to what she is alluding too, Daniel stands motionless, unable to respond.

Disgusted at his reaction, or lack thereof, she continues, "Never mind, Daniel, just let me be." Mary turns back to the computer. "I need time to think this one through. I hope you enjoyed your day in the sun."

"Mary, please listen to me." Daniel pleads. "I swear that I have no idea what happened to me yesterday." At that moment, he notices an image of himself in a mirror behind Mary's desk. He is overwhelmed by the redness of his skin. He walks to the mirror and touches his face. "What the hell is going on?"

Without looking up, Mary replies, "That's what I'd like to know." Mary swivels her chair around and addresses him with anger in her voice. "If this is supposed to be funny, Agent Scudder, I'm not laughing! Nor is anyone else! The chief, Tommy, me, we all worried about what may have happened. Next thing you know, you'll be telling me you were abducted by aliens."

Daniel turns and moves behind the desk. With both hands, he grabs the chair and swings Mary around to face him. He seizes the arms of her chair, leans down and stares into her face.

"Mary, I'm telling you, I don't have a clue as to what the hell happened to me. Now that I think about it, I have no recollection of going home on Monday night." He lets go of the chair. "The last thing I remember is arriving at the Las Vegas airstrip at 2200 hours. I went to my car, got in, and drove home. I can't even remember if I got there. After that, my last memory is of driving to work this morning. I don't remember getting up or even getting ready for work. I just remember being in my car and driving to the airstrip, before taking the shuttle here."

"Is that the best excuse you can come up with?"

"Mary, I swear to you on my life, I don't remember anything about yesterday, absolutely nothing."

They both pause and study each other. The expression on his face convinces Mary there may be some truth to what he is telling her.

"Do you remember the Steddum case and the Maynard's son?" Daniel asks.

Mary is uncertain about his question. "Daniel ... I'm not sure what ..."

He interrupts her. "Remember the time lapse theory? Remember how some of the people we interviewed had periods of time they could not account for?"

Thinking that Daniel is alluding to the idea he had been abducted, she asks with a bit of skepticism, "And your point is?"

Grasping her innuendo, he shouts, "My point is I have no recollection of the last twenty eight hours, or so! None."

Mary realizes the seriousness of his dilemma and tries to calm him. "Daniel, let's not jump to any conclusions. What you're saying is serious. Let's be rational. We need to think clearly about what to do next."

Daniel gets excited. "I want you to hypnotize me."

"This is silly."

"Mary, please! You have to believe me. I don't recall anything about Tuesday. Somewhere, somehow, I lost an entire day. So, where did it go? I haven't a clue. Do you?"

Mary is dumbfounded and offers no response.

"I want to know what is happening to me. How do you explain this ... this redness on my body?"

"I don't know."

"Maybe it's a coincidence, but many of our study subjects have experienced the same type of redness after reporting they were abducted."

"Daniel, there has never been proof ..."

"Listen to me!" Daniel exclaims. He hesitates for a moment while trying to put it all in perspective, then regains his composure. "Mary, I don't know what the hell happened to me yesterday and neither do you, but I've got to find out. Under hypnosis, I might remember something. Perhaps ... I suppose that it is possible ... maybe I am suffering from some sort of amnesia. But amnesia doesn't just happen, so what caused it?"

"Why don't we call Dr. Martin and get his opinion?"

"No. I am not crazy! I'm simply missing a day out of my life."

"Okay, all right. I'll set up the camcorder, but it will take me a minute. Besides, for my own sanity, I need to get my thoughts in order."

Daniel is calmer as he takes her hands in his and kisses them. "Thank you. I'll tell you what; let me take you to lunch."

"I don't know ..."

Daniel pleads, "Mary, please!" He tries to control his frustration. "I need you today more than at any other time in my life. Please, Mary. Come on, we're not talking about the Ritz, we're talking about the compound's cafeteria."

"Okay. Let's have a nice relaxing lunch. You shouldn't be tense before going under hypnosis." Mary examines the reddish hue on his face and hands. "Why don't we go to medical and let the doctor give you a once-over?"

2:15 p.m.

After a leisurely lunch, completely void of any conversation regarding his past disappearance, they visit the medical facility. Mary and Daniel then return to her office and enter the session room. Although most sessions are conducted in the field, there are occasions when someone who has reportedly been abducted is studied on the premises. The determining factor for such a study is based on the hysteria surrounding the case, or to avoid the media.

In these rare cases, where the proclaimed abducted are brought to Area 51, the patient is blindfolded, and then flown to the facility under military supervision. Once the possible abductee has arrived, he or she is escorted to Mary's session room, the door is closed, and guards are posted outside. Then, and only then, is the blindfold removed.

The decor of the session room offers warmth and comfort. Bookshelves span the full length of the wall to the right of the entrance. A large leather sofa occupies the space in the center of the room. An end table with a lamp on it dresses up the sofa at either end. Adjacent to the table at one end of the sofa is an overstuffed executive chair on casters. On this table there has been placed a remote control and a decanter filled with water, which is always present during a session.

At the other end of the sofa, a recliner, also on casters, sits next to the table. A coffee table is positioned three feet in front of the sofa. This allows room for Mary to roll her chair forward while questioning a potential abductee.

A camcorder rests on a tripod about four feet beyond the coffee table, to the left of the doorway that leads into Mary's outer office. The wall behind the tripod is covered with a serene floor-to-ceiling mural of Lake Tahoe. A few feet behind the sofa is a draped window that looks out onto the desolate landscape of the Area 51 compound. The drapes are always drawn when a supposed abductee is on the property.

Mary points to the couch. "Have a seat."

Daniel does as instructed.

Mary adjusts the camcorder. "I know you have seen this routine hundreds of times, but I must tell you, it's different when you are the person undergoing hypnosis."

"I understand, Doc," Daniel responds with a hint of sarcasm in his voice.

"I'm serious, Daniel."

"Yes, Doctor," he replies with a childlike grin.

Mary gives him the stare of death.

Playfully, Daniel continues, "I'm kidding. Remember, this was my idea."

Mary walks to her chair beside the sofa and sits.

Facing Daniel, she issues instructions. "Go ahead and lie down."

"Anything you say, Doc."

Firmly, Mary states, "Get serious, Daniel."

Daniel lies back on the sofa and adjusts his pillow.

"Okay, Doc. Ready whenever you are."

Mary picks up the remote control from the end table and points it toward the camcorder, turning it on. She glances at her watch and begins the session.

"Wednesday, May 17th. The subject, Daniel Scudder, is a 43-year-old male. His profession is that of an investigative agent for a division of the FBI known as the Terrestrials Project. He claims to be suffering from a lapse in memory, dating from about Monday, May 15, 10:00 p.m. to approximately Wednesday, May 17, at 7:30 a.m. In addition to the sudden memory loss, he has developed a red hue that covers his entire body. A medical examination is inconclusive. However, it does not appear to be a burn of any kind. No known elements or dyes were detected in the pigmentation of the skin. Tissue samples taken from the patient ..."

"Patient?" Daniel interrupts her. "Now I'm a *patient*?"

Mary points the remote towards the camcorder and pushes pause.

"Daniel, you do want me to take you seriously, don't you?"

"Well, yes, but ..."

"Then you need to let me conduct this session. I thought you said at lunch that you wanted me to treat you the same as any other patient?"

"I do." Daniel makes a joke. "Actually, I said abductee."

Mary glares at him. "There is no reason to believe you were abducted. You need to get serious. Now relax and let me do my job. For all practical purposes, you are a patient. Do you understand?"

"Yes, but ..."

"No buts! Now, shall we continue?"

"You're the doctor."

"All right then, no more outbursts, or this session is over."

"Yes, ma'am."

Mary points the remote and re-starts the camcorder. "As I was saying, examination of the patient indicates a superficial coloration. There is no burning and no indication of dye or a chemical interaction. Perhaps the cause of the skin discoloration is from a form of ultraviolet light similar to those used in tanning beds."

She turns to Daniel, lying on the sofa. "Daniel, if you are ready, we can begin."

"I'm ready."

Mary places the remote on the table, then picks up a locket from the end table next to her chair and holds it up in front of his face.

"Daniel, I want you to focus on this locket."

Daniel follows the locket with his eyes as she swings it back and forth.

"I need you to relax. Try to clear your mind of all thought. Your eyelids are getting heavy … heavier … heavier. Sleep. Deep, deep sleep."

Daniel lies peacefully on the sofa with his eyes shut.

"Daniel, I want you to remain on the sofa with your eyes closed. Do you understand?"

"Yes."

After placing the locket down on the coffee table, Mary begins her questioning. "Okay, Daniel, I need you to take me back to Monday night, May 15th. Do you remember where you went after you left my office?"

"Yes."

"Tell me, Daniel, where did you go?"

"I drove to the lab at Area 52."

"Why?"

"To drop off a specimen."

"That is where the lab for unidentifiable materials is located?" Mary verifies.

"Yes."

"Did you drop the specimen off?"

"Yes."

"What time did you leave Area 52?"

"At 8:30 p.m."

"Where did you go next?"

"I was running late," Daniel answers, "but I managed to catch the shuttle home. Once I arrived at the Las Vegas airstrip, I got in my car and began to drive to my house."

"What time did you get home?"

"I never got home."

"So where did you go?"

"I'm not sure."

"Daniel, think. You say that you didn't go home?"

"Correct."

"And you were driving?"

"Yes."

"So where did you go?"

Daniel does not answer.

"Can you hear me, Daniel?" Mary asks.

"Yes."

"Well, where did you go?"

"I don't know."

"Daniel, I need for you to recall more about that night. I want you to describe to me what you saw as you were driving."

"I saw stars. They were so bright."

"You saw stars?"

"Yes."

"Daniel?"

"Yes?"

"Did you talk to anyone after you left the airstrip?" Mary becomes exasperated.

"Yes."

"With whom did you speak?"

"The sky."

"You spoke to the sky while driving down the road?"

"Yes."

"What was the conversation about?"

"I talked to the sky."

"I know. So what did you say to the sky?"

"I asked why they have to be so secretive, and what could be gained from watching us. Then, I told the sky that Mary was right, perhaps I have wasted the past fourteen years chasing nothing. I wanted to know where we go from here. How we can prove their existence."

Daniel lies quietly.

Mary prods him, "Did you continue the conversation with yourself?"

"No."

"Where did you drive to?"

Daniel waves his hands in the air. "Nowhere. I just kept driving."

"Daniel, think about it, you had to go somewhere."

"No ... no, I don't think so."

"Well, did you stop for gas?" He pauses again, and she tries to garner a response.

"Daniel?"

Still, he says nothing. Mary changes her question, doing her best to evoke a reply.

"Daniel, did you stop to eat?"

Daniel remains silent as the wind kicks up outside, and a faint glow, or aura, surrounds his body.

She becomes uneasy, but tries again to elicit an answer. "Daniel, can you hear me?"

Finally, Daniel speaks, his voice tinged with exuberance. "It is beautiful!"

"What is beautiful?"

"The light in the sky, it is so mesmerizing!"

"What light, Daniel?"

"It's coming toward me, and I'm not even afraid." Daniel whispers with reverence. "This is what I've waited for my entire life."

"Daniel, are you sure that what you saw was a light? Could it have been a comet?"

"No, it's them!"

"Them who?"

"It's them, Mary. It's the aliens!"

Those words send a chill down Mary's spine. In an instant, Daniel's sudden proclamation invokes fear, uncertainty, and bewilderment in her heart. At a loss as to what to ask next, Mary decides to bring him out of this deep state of hypnosis.

"Daniel, I'm going to count to three ..."

Daniel continues to speak. "They finally chose me."

"When I count to three ..."

"Oh, Mary, they really are here ..."

"... you will awaken."

"I'm here! It's me. I'm right here!"

Mary repeats herself. "One, two, three."

On the word three, the wind dies, and the aura surrounding Daniel's body disappears.

Unaware that he has been in a trance, Daniel opens his eyes and looks at Mary. "Well, I'm ready when you are."

Surprised by his comment, Mary picks up the remote off the table, points it in the direction of the camcorder, and turns it off.

"It's over, Daniel."

Daniel is confused. "What's over?"

"This session is over."

"Mary, I promise, I won't say another word. Go ahead, do your thing."

Concerned about what has just taken place, Mary tells Daniel, "I think I would like Dr. Martin to sit in on our next session."

Daniel queries, "I thought we talked about this?"

"Honey, I know. It's ... well ... we're so close, I think it would be best if we had an unbiased opinion when I put you under hypnosis."

"Are you still mad at me?" Daniel asks, uncertain of Mary's mindset.

Mary strokes his face with her hand as though he was a child. "No, Honey, not at all."

CHAPTER 3
The Soul of Man

THURSDAY, MAY 18th - 9:00 a.m.

Dr. Martin, a pudgy, brown skinned, gray haired and bearded man in his sixties, fumbles through the paperwork on his cluttered, over-sized desk. Mary sits across from him in a chair on the opposite side.

Unable to find whatever he is looking for, Dr. Martin stops for a moment before continuing. "I'm sorry, Agent Drake, what can I do for you today?"

"Actually, it's what you can do for Agent Scudder."

"What seems to be the problem, my dear?" the doctor asks as he continues shuffling his papers.

"You know, Dr. Martin, I have been diagnosing the alleged abducted for almost fourteen years."

"Yes, my dear, I am familiar with your work. I've had the privilege of studying a few of your past sessions."

"I know. That's why I came to you."

"Does Agent Scudder doubt your analysis again?"

"No, it's nothing like that. Actually, I put Agent Scudder under hypnosis yesterday. That's why I'm here."

Dr. Martin stops shuffling his papers and focuses on the conversation. "And what was the reason for his hypnosis?"

Mary explains the situation. "Daniel, that is, Agent Scudder, didn't show up for work on Tuesday. It appears as though he is suffering from some kind of memory loss. He has no recollection of what happened the entire day."

"Maybe he wanted to escape the madness for a change. Isn't it possible that he does recall but doesn't want you or anyone else to know what he was up to?"

"I thought the same thing, at first, but now I'm not sure what to think."

"What do you mean?"

Mary removes a flash drive from her purse and hands it to Dr. Martin. "I would like your opinion about this video. It's my session with Agent Scudder."

"Okay, I'll try and sneak it in before I leave this evening."

"Dr. Martin, I would appreciate it if you could view it as soon as possible."

He notices an expression of concern on her face. "May I ask why?"

"He thinks he was abducted."

Dr. Martin chuckles. "Well, Agent Drake, why do you find that so hard to believe?"

"Pardon?"

"We are all aware of Agent Scudder's enthusiasm when it comes to extraterrestrials. Is that what Agent Scudder revealed to you during this session?"

"Yes, Doctor."

"Agent Drake, my dear, you of all people should know he is probably fantasizing under hypnosis about what he would love to believe in his conscious state."

"Yes, I know, and normally I would agree. I mean, I do agree. It's just that … maybe I'm too close to Daniel to offer a fair and objective diagnosis." She stands and paces the room. "I've analyzed hundreds of so-called abductees. Ninety percent of their stories are similar, and all of them, while under hypnosis, admit they have heard about abductions from one source of the media or another."

Dr. Martin observes from her pacing that Mary is troubled by this event. "So, what makes Agent Scudder different? After all, he has heard all of their stories, seen all of the related press, and read every report."

"Yes, but this time it is different. A glow, an aura, if you will, surrounded him while he was under. Then, as soon as I brought him out of the trance, it vanished."

"Agent Drake, I'm sure there is a reasonable explanation."

She leans back in the chair. "I know, Dr. Martin. I'm sure you are right. But I would feel better about this if you would sit in on our next session. You see, in all of the years I have known Scudder; he has never lied to me. I realize he is human and that he is no different from anyone else whom I have analyzed in the past. Nonetheless, it's hard for me to accept that he could invent such a story in his subconscious. Besides, it's a little troubling that he said my name while in his hypnotic state. It was as if he was making sure I knew he was aware of my presence."

"Creating a story while in the subconscious is not the same as telling a lie in a conscious state. And though it is unusual for someone to acknowledge another person in the present state while under hypnosis, you might be reading more into it than you need to." Dr. Martin perceives the troubled expression on her face. "Well, if it bothers you that much, I suppose I could rearrange my schedule. Meanwhile, I will take a look at the tape before the session. What time did you have in mind?"

"I've scheduled his next session for 1600 hours."

"That's fine, my dear, I'll be there."

"Thank you." She walks to the door. "If you don't mind, Dr. Martin ..."

Dr. Martin glances up as he begins shuffling through his paperwork, again. "Yes, my dear?"

"Please don't mention the tape to Agent Scudder. He doesn't recall being hypnotized yesterday. That is what troubles me the most."

"Okay, if that's how you prefer to handle it. But, my dear, I wouldn't worry too much about his recollection. After all, there are many known cases of a patient not recalling a session. Perhaps Scudder has buried his story in his subconscious to protect himself from ridicule."

"I'm sure you're right. Thank you, Dr. Martin."

4:10 p.m.

Dr. Martin apologizes as he enters the session room in Mary's office. "I'm sorry I couldn't get here sooner."

Mary points to a seat. "No problem, Dr. Martin. Agent Scudder is also running behind. He should be here any moment."

Though the sun is shining outside, the closed blackout drapes hanging on the windows behind the sofa prevent any light from shining in. The only lighting in the room comes from the lamp on the end table next to Dr. Martin. Mary is sitting in her chair at the other end of the couch, facing Dr. Martin.

"I had a chance to go over the video a few minutes ago. To be honest with you, Agent Drake, I did not find Scudder's behavior any more unusual than the average person who claims to have been abducted."

"I would normally agree, Dr. Martin, but it's what I felt and saw during the session that throws me. I guess it's ... I don't know ... something about ... well ... the excitement he exhibited about the light in the sky was quite convincing. And then there was the aura surrounding his body."

"Come on, Drake. I have seen dozens of your sessions where patients become excited at the fantasy of alien abduction. As for the aura, I noticed the drapes behind the sofa appeared to be a bit separated. It appeared to be a glare coming in from the outside."

"Perhaps you're right. Like I stated in your office, maybe I'm too close to offer a fair diagnosis."

Daniel arrives. Harried, he taps on the door as he pushes it open.

"Hello. Sorry I'm late." He enters the room.

Mary answers, "That's okay. Dr. Martin and I were discussing various case studies from the past."

"Trying to decide which nutcase to compare me to, huh? I dare to think what you might say if it's revealed under hypnosis that I was abducted."

Daniel's remark validates he does not recall having been placed under hypnosis the day before. Mary and Dr. Martin glance at each other but say nothing.

Without direction, Daniel advances to the sofa and reclines the full length of it. He places a pillow under his head and says in a jovial voice, "Well, no need to hold up the inevitable. Shall we get down to business?"

Dr. Martin concurs, "Absolutely," while studying Daniel's demeanor.

Mary rolls her chair closer to the sofa.

She points the remote at the camcorder and pushes start.

Looking into the camera's lens, she dictates her preamble. "Thursday, May 18th, session two, with Special Agent Daniel Scudder."

Mary chooses her words carefully to avoid any suspicion that Daniel may have regarding his last session.

"Unable to find a reasonable explanation for Agent Scudder's memory loss, I have asked Dr. Martin from the Psychology Division of the Terrestrials Project to participate as an observer. Agent Scudder, if you and Dr. Martin are ready we can begin."

Mary picks up the locket off the end table, leans forward, and slowly swings it back and forth in front of Daniel's face.

"Daniel, follow the locket with your eyes. I need you to clear your mind of all thoughts. Your eyelids are getting heavy. Heavy and heavier. You are getting sleepy."

Daniel closes his eyes.

"Daniel, are you asleep?" Mary asks.

"Yes."

Mary leans back in her chair and places the locket on the table beside her. "Daniel, you will keep your eyes closed until I count to three. On the count of three, you will awaken. Do you understand?"

"Yes."

Mary offers him a reminder. "Daniel, in our last session you were telling me about Tuesday, May 16th. Do you remember?"

"No. I'm not sure."

"Daniel, think back to the evening of Tuesday, May 16th. Can you do that?"

"I'm trying to remember ..."

"Do you remember driving home from the airstrip?"

"Yes."

"Do you remember seeing a light in the sky?"

Daniel hesitates, then exclaims, "Yes! They are here, Mary! They really are here!"

Mary and Dr. Martin both jump as something bangs against the building outside. Unaffected by the sound, Daniel lies perfectly still on the sofa.

Dr. Martin gets up from his chair, walks around to the window, and peers through the drapes. He sees a dark and ominous-looking cloud racing in from over the mountains.

Calmly Dr. Martin remarks, "It appears a springtime storm is brewing."

He closes the drapes and returns to his chair.

Mary and the doctor notice that a faint glow has begun to surround Daniel's body as he lays patiently, waiting for the next question.

"Who's here, Daniel?" Mary asks.

"The aliens."

"And where are you?"

"I'm right here, under their ship."

"What ship?"

"It's magnificent, Mary. It's unlike anything we could have ever imagined."

"What do you mean, Daniel?"

"The colors, they are so beautiful. It's so quiet, Mary. There is no sound at all, just total serenity."

Daniel's face radiates with excitement as the wind rages outside.

Doing her best to ignore the commotion outside, Mary proceeds, "Are you still under the craft?"

"Yes."

"Daniel, tell me, what is happening now?"

"It's opening. I'm floating. My car is floating upward."

"Where is the car going, Daniel?"

"Nowhere, just up." He pauses as if waiting for something. "The car is inside the spacecraft now. It is so huge, Mary. It's like a giant, floating city."

Daniel lies motionless in total silence.

Mary coaxes him to keep talking. "Go on, Daniel, tell me what you see."

"The hatch to the ship has closed." Daniel hesitates for a moment. "I think we are moving. It's difficult to tell."

"Can you explain?"

"There are no windows, and the movement is almost imperceptible."

Daniel grows quiet.

"Daniel?"

"Yes?"

"I need for you to tell me what is happening."

"Okay. I am getting out of the car. I see a bright light. It's so intense, I can hardly see." He pauses.

"Go on."

"A passageway has opened. A voice ..."

"Yes, Daniel?"

Daniel takes his time to explain, while Mary and Dr. Martin listen with anticipation of what he will say next.

"The voice is directing me down a long corridor. I have reached the end of the hall. Now a door has opened into an adjoining room."

"What is inside the room?"

"As best I can tell, medical equipment. The voice has directed me to disrobe. I am laying my clothes across a bench." Suddenly, Daniel throws his arms up across his face, and without opening his eyes, he shouts as if in agony, "Ahhh!"

"What's going on, Daniel? What is happening to you?"

"The light."

"What about the light?"

"It's much brighter than before. It hurts my eyes." He abruptly moves his hands from his eyes and covers his ears. "Ahhh! The sound is so loud!"

Mary is alarmed and concerned at his reaction. "Daniel, are you all right?"

In an instant, he relaxes, placing his arms by his sides. "Yes. The sound and the light have stopped."

"What is the purpose for the sound and the light?"

"To kill the harmful bacteria and germs that

cover my body."

"The aliens told you that?"

"No." Daniel runs his fingers through his prematurely silver hair, and then places his hands back to his sides. "Somehow I just know."

"Daniel, what is happening now?"

"A door is opening, they're coming toward me."

"Who are, they?"

"The aliens. The extraterrestrials."

He appears peaceful as he lies on the sofa.

The aura surrounding his body intensifies. Mary and Dr. Martin look first at each other, then at Daniel. Due to the storm outside, darkness pervades the room.

Mary moves her chair back enough to switch on the lamp on the end table next to her. Stillness invades the room, except for the sound of the wind howling ferociously outside the window. The heavenly glow that surrounds Daniel's body grows brighter. An eerie presence besieges the room as if Mary and Dr. Martin were conducting a séance. With apprehension and uncertainty, Mary moves her chair back in place beside the sofa.

Mary encourages him, "Go on, Daniel, what happened next?"

Daniel continues as though he is speaking to someone else. "Hello, my name is Daniel Scudder. I am an agent for the FBI."

"Daniel?" Mary asks.

"Yes?"

"As you tell me what you say and do, can you also describe to me how the extraterrestrials respond?"

Daniel is gleeful. "Sure."

"So, tell me, Daniel, how did they reply when you told them who you were?"

Daniel converses with himself. His voice alternates between the one that Mary recognizes and a low monotone, as if one of the aliens was speaking.

"Yes, we know who you are," Daniel replies in this strange voice.

He weeps with excitement.

Mary and Dr. Martin look at each other.

With fearful fascination, Mary whispers to the doctor, "I think I should wake him."

Dr. Martin quietly answers, "No, no, he appears to be fine. This is a form of delusion. Let's continue for a few more minutes."

Suddenly, and without Mary's prodding, Daniel speaks in his normal voice. "You have no idea how I have longed for this day."

"Come. Come with us." The unidentifiable voice makes a request.

"Wow! This place is beyond imagination. So, may I ask you a few questions?"

"Is that not why you are here?"

"Well, yes, but really I am here because you abducted me." Daniel pauses, as if waiting for laughter. "Some people would find that humorous." He lies on the sofa as if waiting for a response, and then says, "Okay. Is this an operating room?"

"Operating room? Oh, yes, I suppose you could call this our operating room. Please sit here. Now, if you will please lie back."

"What is this thing that you are putting on my head?"

"It is nothing to worry about. Please do not be frightened."

"Oh, no, I can assure you I'm not frightened at all. But I am curious as to what you are doing. Why did you have me disrobe?"

"You have been trying to discover us for a long time now. What do you hope to gain from your quest?"

"I hope to find an explanation as to why you are observing us. What's that? No, no!"

"What do you see, Daniel?" Mary asks.

"Ah!" he screams. "What the hell did you do that for?"

Mary becomes anxious. "Daniel, Daniel, what is going on?"

"They ran a probe up my nose. Ah! Shit!"

He grabs his crotch and yells, "Now they're running a probe up my dick!"

"Daniel, I want you to tell me, step-by-step, what is happening. Everything they say."

Daniel continues this strange conversation.

"You may sit up and get dressed. Do you know who you are?"

"Well, yes, I told you, I am FBI Agent, Daniel Scudder."

"Yes, but do you know the whole of you?"

"What do you mean?"

"The physical being is Daniel Scudder, but the soul of you is not the same."

"I'm not sure I understand."

"Every living thing has a spirit. The spirit manifests based upon every experience each soul has."

"I don't understand."

"When a living thing dies, a blade of grass, a tree, an insect, an animal, any living thing, given the right circumstances, that energy will attach itself to another living being. With each successive iteration, that energy grows stronger. As time passes, if that energy sustains itself and becomes strong enough, it will manifest into a soul, an energy we believe has the potential to live forever, if cared for. The human soul is an accumulation of all those experiences, a manifestation of all living things. With each reincarnation of the soul, the energy, or essence of that being becomes wiser and greater."

"To be clear, our souls are made up of the memories, or experiences, of all of the living things that we may have come in contact with from the past?"

"That is correct. Do you remember your grandmother?"

"Yes."

"This is she, her essence."

Daniel grows silent, and Mary becomes concerned.

"Daniel, are you all right? Can you hear me?"

Without acknowledging her, Daniel continues to speak.

"Grandma, it really is you."

A tear streams down his face.

Confused, Mary inquires, "Daniel, do you see your grandmother?"

"Yes, she is a ball of light. She is inside this crystal-like object, a bright, white light, like a ball of energy. So, this is what it's like, this is your soul.

Daniel continues his conversation with himself. "Wait. Where are you going? Where are you taking her?"

"We must prepare her soul for its next host."

"Will I know her in that new host?"

"Yes. She will always be a part of you. She will always be with you. Like souls often travel together throughout eternity."

"Can you tell me how I will recognize her in the flesh?"

"Her soul will soon be transformed into another life form. As a new-man of Earth, you will not know her presence by the flesh, but you will feel a kinship to her soul, similar to when you feel that you have known a person forever. The shell, or host, is how we feel, how we love, and how we learn. We exist in the flesh, but the soul is who we are, past and present."

Highly concerned, Mary looks at Dr. Martin. "I'm bringing him out of this, now! Daniel, I am going to count to three ..."

Dr. Martin throws out a hand to stop her. "Mary, I think that we should let him ..."

Mary cuts him off. "Daniel, when I count to three, you will awaken."

Daniel acts as though he does not hear her.

He continues his conversation with the alien. "I

have so many questions. Where do I begin?"

Mary brings Daniel out of hypnosis. "One, two, three."

On the count of three, the wind outside subsides, and the aura surrounding Daniel's body disappears. He abruptly opens his eyes.

She points the remote toward the recorder and turns it off. Mary approaches the window and opens the drapes. She is astounded to see the sun is shining and not a cloud in the sky.

In the meantime, Daniel sits up and rubs his face as if awakening from a deep sleep.

Troubled, Mary returns to the sofa and sits next to him.

She pours Daniel a glass of water from the decanter on the end table. "Daniel, are you okay?"

Daniel is still groggy. "Yes, I'm fine. What happened? I'm exhausted."

Daniel takes a drink from the glass.

Mary is sympathetic. "Why don't you lie here for a while and rest. I have a couple of things to discuss with Dr. Martin before we leave."

"Okay." Daniel lies back down on the couch.

Mary and Dr. Martin both stand and leave the room, closing the door to the session room behind them. Once in her outer office, she and Dr. Martin converse.

"What happened in there?" Mary asks.

"I don't know." Dr. Martin rubs his mostly bald head. "If I were a Catholic, I would say that we need to call in an exorcist. I've heard of many cases of delusion in my years as a psychologist, but none quite like this."

"Where did he come up with all of this business about the soul?" Mary shakes her head, "And his grandmother. I've rarely heard him even mention his grandmother, certainly not in that context. And how do you explain the voice alterations?"

Dr. Martin tries to make sense of it all. "Agent Drake, have you ever discussed religion with Agent Scudder?"

"Yes, but very seldom. In fact, it's a subject that he feels somewhat uncomfortable talking about."

"I'm aware of his studies in theology, but does he declare himself an atheist?"

"No. Daniel definitely believes in a higher being. I guess the best way to describe him is agnostic. Although he is well versed in the Bible, he finds it to be somewhat obscure. He believes religion is a tool, created and written by man as a way to control, just as man creates laws by which to govern."

Dr. Martin ponders aloud. "I'm going to do some investigating into Scudder's past relationships with his family members, particularly his grandmother. I'm sure Daniel is fine. He probably misses his grandmother more than his conscious wants to admit. Perhaps he is having a problem letting go."

"But, Dr. Martin, his grandparents have been dead for more than twenty years. Of that much I am certain."

"It's possible that he's been carrying this baggage around for all of these years, and this is his way of letting go."

"Yes, but Dr. Martin, what does all of this have to do with his whereabouts on Tuesday, May 16th? I thought that is what we are trying to determine. And how do you explain the aura that surrounded his body?"

"I'm not sure what to conclude right now. When can you schedule Agent Scudder for another session?"

"When you have an agent in charge of interviewing reported abductees believing that he himself was abducted, I would think that scheduling another session should take precedence over everything else."

"I couldn't concur more, my dear."

"I'll set up a session for this time tomorrow. And, Dr. Martin ..."

"Yes, my dear?"

"I don't feel Daniel should be privy to what we've learned so far, at least not until we can put together some kind of a plausible explanation for all of this."

"I agree. I will rearrange my schedule around tomorrow's session. In the interim, my dear, do not dwell on this. Whatever is troubling Agent Scudder, I'm sure we'll be able to determine the source. Let us take this one-step at a time. I'll see you tomorrow."

"Thank you, Dr. Martin. I'll see you then."

Mary rejoins Daniel in the session room. Upon entering, Mary sees him standing behind the camcorder looking into the viewer lens.

"Daniel! What are you doing?"

Embarrassed at having been caught, Daniel stammers, "What? You ... you scared me!"

She approaches the camcorder and turns it off. "It would be best if you didn't review your own session. So how much did you see?"

"Nothing," he replies, sheepishly.

Mary stares at him in disbelief.

"I mean, I know you asked me questions about my whereabouts, and something about a light in the sky." Daniel notices a shocked look on her face and wonders what she is hiding. "Mary, is there something you wish to tell me? I mean, according to this video, you placed me under hypnosis in the first session, yet, you led me to believe the opposite. What is going on? Moreover, try telling the truth, please. I am a big boy. I can handle it. Whatever *it* is."

"Daniel, I think it would be best to save your questions for later. At least, until Dr. Martin and I can make some sense of your condition."

"My condition? What the hell does that mean?"

Mary grabs Daniel's arm and leads him to the couch. "Daniel, do you trust me?"

"Of course."

"Then please let me handle this. I love you, and you know that everything I do is in your best interest."

"I know, and I'm okay with that, for now. Just answer me one question, and I won't pry any further."

"If I can."

"Did I tell you where I was on Tuesday?"

"All I will tell you is that you offered an explanation."

Gently, she brushes a strand of hair away from his forehead. At that instant, a trickle of blood drips from his nose. Mary reaches for a tissue.

CHAPTER 4
Unexpected Light

7:30 p.m.

Daniel enters Mary's office and finds her sitting at her computer working on a report.

"Honey, are you ready?" He kisses the nape of her neck.

"Give me a few more minutes."

Daniel glances at the computer screen and sees his name. "Hey, that's me you're writing about."

Mary puts her hand in front of the computer. "Daniel, I'm typing in today's session report. Now go away."

"Can't I see it?"

"No, Daniel. I never allow anyone to see their reports."

"Yes, but you don't sleep with them."

"True. But the answer is still no."

"Okay. Have it your way. I hope it's interesting. I would hate to think I'm a bore."

"Daniel, I told you," she pushes him away, "I'll be done in a couple of minutes. Now go."

He walks over to the sofa, and Mary turns back to the computer to finish her report. He picks up a magazine and impatiently riffles through it, sighing several times.

Mary stops typing and turns toward him. He deliberately holds the magazine in front of his face so as not to look at her.

Mary turns back to the computer and shuts it down. "I think I'll finish this tomorrow."

Daniel peers from behind the magazine. "You don't have to stop on my account. I promise, I'll just sit here quietly and finish this article in *Sports Illustrated*."

Knowing that the only magazine on her coffee table is not a *Sports Illustrated*, Mary retorts, "It's *Cosmopolitan*."

"What?"

Annoyed, she gathers her briefcase and purse. She ambles to where he sits.

"The magazine you are reading is *Cosmopolitan*, not *Sports Illustrated*."

Daniel reviews the cover. "Oh, so it is."

"Come on. Let's go." She playfully bonks the top of his head.

With a grin on his face, like a kid who gets his way, Daniel replaces the magazine on the table, and follows her.

After leaving her office, they board the commuter plane from the Area 51 compound to the Las Vegas airstrip. Upon their arrival, Daniel's car is brought around. It's getting late, and Mary decides it's best that Daniel spends the night at her place. While driving home, both of their thoughts are on the past days' events. Twenty minutes pass without a word spoken. They reach the turn-off to the lonely stretch of highway that takes them to Mary's house. The desert is pitch-black, with the exception of the moon and the stars illuminating the sky.

Daniel breaks the silence. "Babe, you aren't angry with me for making us leave, are you?"

"No, not at all. It was getting late, anyway, and I have a lot on my mind."

"I'm sorry. So, how did your day go, other than your session with me?"

"Fine. The chief may be sending us to New Mexico. We'll be interviewing a woman who claims she was taken aboard an alien craft back in March."

"Yes, I heard. He briefly mentioned her to me prior to his leaving this afternoon."

Mary gazes out her car window and notices a series of bright lights dancing behind a small mound just off the road in the desert. It is the same mound where the family of four experienced their unsettling encounter several days earlier.

Unaware of Mary's observation, Daniel says, "I know you get tired of our trips, always having to lug that camera around, listening to one strange tale after another."

Mary's obliviousness captures his attention. Daniel glances over to see if she is all right. He notices the lights out in the desert but says nothing.

Just as they are about to pass the mound, while still looking into the desert, Mary declares, "Daniel, pull over!"

Daniel parks the car on the side of the road and shuts off the engine. He removes a flashlight and his gun holster from the glove box. Upon exiting the car, they cautiously walk toward the mound.

"What do you think it is?" Daniel asks.

Mary is intent on moving forward. "I can't tell, but it's too bright to be a reflection of the moon or the stars."

As they approach, the lights disappear. They stop and look at each other. Suddenly, without a sound, a solid black object takes off from behind the mound at an excessive speed. The obstacle is so huge that it stirs up a swirling gust of wind that nearly knocks them off their feet. The sand-filled dust devil causes them to blink, making it difficult to focus.

"Did you see that?" Daniel questions with excitement.

"See what?"

Daniel is uncertain too. "Well, I don't know exactly." He hesitates a moment. "I didn't hear anything, did you?"

"No, I didn't."

An eerie feeling overcomes her. It is the same feeling she felt while Daniel was under hypnosis. She fights to keep fear from taking over.

Feeling uneasy, she appeals to Daniel. "Come on."

Again, they cautiously move toward the mound. Out in the darkness, a low growling sound wafts on the cool night air. Both stop to listen.

Mary whispers, "What was that?"

"I don't know," Daniel quietly answers back.

He flips on the flashlight and shines it toward the mound. In a laggard motion, he moves the light back and forth. From out of nowhere, the face of a tiger appears in the path of the light. Daniel holds the flashlight on the tiger's face, not believing what he sees. The tiger growls as if ready to attack.

Daniel gently suggests to Mary, "Back up slowly."

Carefully, they trek backwards in the direction of the car. Without warning, the tiger pounces. Daniel drops the light and reaches for his gun. Losing sight of the tiger, they turn toward the car.

Daniel shouts, "Run!"

Grabbing Mary's hand, they scramble. She glances back long enough to see the flashlight, still shining, lying on the ground.

Daniel vehemently insists, "Don't look back! Keep running!"

Frantically, they climb inside the vehicle, close the doors and lock them. Mary catches a glimpse of a light as she locks her door. Though it is only for a few brief seconds, another glance reveals that the glow from the flashlight has disappeared into the side of the mound.

Completely unaware of Mary's observation, Daniel starts the car and drives away.

He is bemused. "What do you make of that?"

"I'm not sure." Mary is dazed and confused.

"And where did that tiger come from?"

"I don't know." Mary pats her hair into place.

While Daniel drives, they sit in silence, pondering what just happened. Curiosity compels Mary to look out her window. High above them, she notices a light in the sky streak by going in the opposite direction. Anxiously, she peers out of the rear window, but observes only darkness.

Daniel senses Mary's uneasiness. "Are you all right?"

"Yes. Sure, I'll be fine. I'm a little shaken, that's all."

While Daniel talks, Mary gazes into the passenger side mirror and realizes the light has reappeared. She rolls down her window and sticks her head out in order to look out and up in the direction of the anomaly. The light hovers steadily behind them.

Concerned, but unaware of her new sighting, Daniel remarks, "I hope whatever I've been telling you under hypnosis has nothing to do with this."

Mary fails to respond as she observes the aberration. In an instant, the light disappears. She pulls her head inside and rolls up the window. Daniel notices her fidgetiness and that her attention is to the passenger side mirror. He adjusts the rearview mirror in an effort to see what she is looking at.

Daniel realizes she didn't hear his last question.

"What's going on with me? I don't suppose that now would be a good time to talk about it, would it?."

Mary speaks in a matter-of-fact tone. "No, Daniel, it wouldn't."

CHAPTER 5
The Beginning

FRIDAY - 3:45 p.m.

Carrying an oversized envelope, Dr. Martin arrives at Mary's outer office. After a cordial greeting, Mary escorts him into the session room.

"I have in this envelope the MRI results from Dr. Jacob's examination of Daniel on Wednesday. You may find them to be of interest."

Mary follows the doctor as he saunters toward the window and opens the curtain, allowing in the sunlight.

Mary becomes intrigued as Dr. Martin removes a negative from the envelope and places it against the window, providing a lighted backdrop.

"You have my attention, Doctor."

Dr. Martin removes a pen from his pocket and uses it as a pointer. "Daniel is as healthy as a horse. Nonetheless, this spot, right here within the left nasal cavity ..."

Mary examines the film. "Yes?"

Dr. Martin circles the blemish on the x-ray with

his pen. "There appears to be a rather miniscule abnormality right here."

They both carefully try to determine its origin as Mary asks, "What is it?"

"Dr. Jacob is not sure, but it doesn't seem to be attached to anything. The doctor suggests it is a foreign compound deliberately placed inside his nasal cavity. You can see the track of disrupted tissue leading to the object. Given Daniel has no record of prior surgeries; how it got there is a mystery. However, it does appear to have been implanted recently, which would account for his nosebleeds. Fortunately, whatever it is, it shouldn't give him any problems."

"Dr. Martin, do you remember what Daniel mentioned under hypnosis?" Mary twists her hands together, noticing the conspicuous absence of an engagement ring.

"About the instrument the so-called aliens stuck up his nose?"

"Yes."

"My dear, In my opinion, Daniel is acting out his greatest fantasy."

"What does that have to do with the unknown substance lodged in his nose?"

Dr. Martin puts his pen away and places the film back in its envelope. "If a person believes in something long and hard enough, they will do anything to make it true. I don't think Daniel is even aware of all he is doing to convince us he was abducted."

"Are you suggesting Daniel deliberately placed something up his nose?

"My dear, I'm not suggesting anything. I am merely presenting the facts as we know them to be."

"But what about the redness to his skin? How do you account for that?"

"I believe it to be an allergic reaction to an ultraviolet light, similar to those used in a tanning booth. Most likely, he wasn't subjected to it long enough to get a burn. But without question, the light did cause a discoloration to his skin."

"I don't know. At first, I came to the same conclusion, but this whole episode with Daniel has me imagining things too."

"How so, my dear?"

"Driving home last night, a series of lights loomed off in the distance. They appeared to be coming from behind a mound in the middle of the desert. Out of curiosity, we stopped to investigate, and as we approached, inexplicably the lights disappeared. As we stood in the dark, Daniel and I thought that we saw something take off from behind the mound, although, we couldn't make out what it was. Then, out of nowhere, a tiger appeared."

"My dear, do you know how strange all of this sounds?"

Mary is becoming annoyed with Dr. Martin's constant referral to her as 'my dear', but she refrains from mentioning it, for now. "Yes, I do."

"Are you sure that what you saw wasn't a reflection from the moon or the stars? From the position from which you observed this mysterious illumination, perhaps it merely appeared to be lights. That would account for why the reflections seemingly disappeared as you approached the mound."

"I arrived at the same conclusion, at first. However, shortly thereafter, as we were driving away, a light abruptly reappeared in the sky above us. It, too, disappeared just as quickly."

"Agent Drake, my dear, the desert can generate as much of an illusion, or a mirage, at night as it does during the day."

"That may be true, but what about the tiger?"

"My dear, I would like to suggest that what you saw may have been a coyote or some other animal roaming around in the desert. In the darkness, it would be difficult to tell."

"I know what I saw, Dr. Martin!"

Dr. Martin tries to reason with her. "My dear, I would like to suggest that this whole episode with Agent Scudder may be affecting your deductive reasoning. I am confident there is a logical explanation for everything you have described."

"I know you're right. It's just that ... I guess what troubles me, other than last night, is Daniel's fantasy under hypnosis. The details are more descriptive than any I have ever heard before. Then there's the distorted voice, the aura, and the unexpected storms."

"It is obvious to me the wind is due to nothing more than an isolated springtime storm. You know how unpredictable the weather can be this time of year. Moreover, the aura, well, that is most likely an illusion generated by the discoloration of his skin. My dear, Daniel is an intelligent man. Despite the way he downplays his intelligence, I understand his I.Q. is off the charts: somewhere in the neighborhood of 163, as I recall. Nonetheless, the man's thought process is all over the map." The doctor glances down at his notes. "He graduated high school at fourteen and college at eighteen with multiple degrees: theology, Egyptology, various sciences, history, math ... it seems like I'm leaving something out."

"Archeology."

"Oh, yes. How could I forget archeology? Despite his bumbling antics, and his obsession with finding UFOs, the man is a walking encyclopedia. We all know how his imagination can run wild."

"Dr. Martin, are you suggesting he is using the knowledge he has acquired over our years of investigating those who claim to have been abducted, and weaving it into some kind of a scenario to convince himself that aliens *do* exist? But why?"

"I prefer to withhold any further thoughts at this time. And by the way, you were right. Both of his grandmothers passed away more than twenty years ago. I spoke with several of his relatives in an attempt to get a better understanding of Agent Scudder's psychological profile."

"Doctor, are you sure you should have involved

them?"

"Don't worry, my dear, I convinced them I was merely conducting a routine profile on a fellow agent. I discovered he was indeed close to his grandparents, particularly his maternal grandmother. I think we may be on the right track."

Mary checks her watch. "Well, it's time. Daniel should be here any minute. If you'll excuse me, Doctor, I need to prepare the video camera."

While Mary adjusts the camcorder, Dr. Martin places the x-ray envelope beside the end table next to his chair, then sits, awaiting Daniel's arrival. Daniel taps on the door.

"Hello." He pokes his head in the doorway. "Sorry, no aliens, it's little ole me."

Mary glances toward the door. "Come on in."

Dr. Martin stands and straightens his tie. "Yes, Agent Scudder, come on in and have a seat on the sofa. We've been preparing for you."

"Don't mind if I do. In fact, I'll go ahead and lie down." He lies back and positions the pillow under his head, then remarks with a bit of sarcasm, "There, all ready. Oh, I'm sorry, you two go on preparing for … exactly what is it that we are preparing for? Oh yeah, right, me."

"Scudder, you are out of line." Mary scolds Daniel, embarrassed by this mini outburst.

Dr. Martin interrupts her. "That's all right, Drake. Agent Scudder has every right to be angry. After all, we know everything he reveals to us under hypnosis, yet, he has no recollection of what he has shared. I am sure that he would like to know what the big secret is."

"Yes, as a matter a fact, I would. I know that these sessions must be pretty intense, or you would have told me something by now."

Dr. Martin offers a suggestion. "Let us get through this session, and we'll see if it's safe enough to talk about."

Insulted by his comment, Daniel sits up. "Safe enough to talk about? I am not an idiot!"

Mary interjects, "Daniel, please. Once we complete this session, we might be able to tell you something more conclusive."

Dr. Martin takes his seat, ignoring Daniel's minor fit of temper.

Daniel lies back on the sofa. "Okay, then, let's get started."

Mary sits in her chair and rolls it next to Daniel. She touches his arm. "I need you to relax."

Using the remote, Mary starts the camcorder. "Friday, May 19th, 4:00 p.m. Session three with Agent Daniel Scudder. We will attempt to pick up where we left off in session two."

Mary picks up the locket and begins to swing it slowly back and forth in front of Daniel's face. "Daniel, I want you to follow the locket with your eyes. Your eyelids are getting heavier and heavier. You can barely hold your eyes open. You are getting sleepier and sleepier; your eyelids are so heavy that you cannot open them. Daniel, are you asleep?"

"Yes."

"Daniel, I need you to remain on the sofa with your eyes closed until I count to three. On the count of three, you will awaken. Do you understand?"

"Yes."

Mary places the locket on the table next to her chair. "Daniel, in our last session you took us on a trip into the sky. Do you remember?"

"Yes."

"Do you remember telling me about your grandmother?"

"Yes."

"You were telling me about her soul. Do you recall that conversation?"

Daniel does not respond.

Mary asks again, "Daniel, do you remember talking about your grandmother?"

Again, he calmly answers, "Yes."

"You said the aliens told you, 'we exist in the flesh, but the soul is who we are.' Do you recall those words?"

All at once, an aura surrounds Daniel's body, and the wind kicks up outside.

"I did not say that, the alien did."

Dr. Martin studies Mary's face as she questions Daniel, but she does not acknowledge this.

"Who is this alien?"

Daniel does not hesitate. "He is The Great Explorer."

Mary glances over at Dr. Martin for his reaction to this statement. It's obvious he is as perplexed as she is.

Mary turns back to Daniel. "Explorer? He told you that?"

"Yes," Daniel rejoins, as though Mary should have already known the answer to the question.

Puzzled, Mary issues instructions. "Daniel, I need you to explain. I want you to go back to the day you visited the alien craft. Tell me, step-by-step, what was said after the aliens took your grandmother away."

"They did not take my grandmother away," he replies. "It was her essence."

Mary pacifies him. "That's right, Daniel, and what happened next?"

She waits patiently for a response. Then, just as she is about to ask again, Daniel speaks. Once more, he carries on the conversation with himself in two different voices. It is as if two people are inside of him.

"I feel as though I know you."

"You do," the alternate voice responds. *"As do I know you. We are as one."*

"What do you mean?"

Daniel sinks deeper and deeper into a trance. He becomes oblivious to the session room. He has no awareness of Mary or Dr. Martin's presence. In this dreamlike state, he envisions himself onboard the alien spacecraft. There, he is seated across from the alien, face-to-face. Mary and Dr. Martin sit back and take note as Daniel converses with this physical being, now sitting before him in his mind, as he shifts between his voice and an eerie rendition of the alien's voice.

"You are one of the many souls that are of us."

"How do you mean?"

"You are, in the physical, that of man. That is, the man known to Earth. However, your soul is one of ours."

"Are you suggesting I'm an alien?"

"Your soul is what some would term as alien, yes."

The alien pauses and observes Daniel's expressions. Although Daniel does not respond, the alien is aware of Daniel's confusion.

The alien continues. *"Perhaps it would be best if I explained from the beginning."*

"The beginning of what?"

"The beginning of humankind, Earth's mankind. Before exploring your solar system, we occupied various regions of what you on Earth call The Milky Way Galaxy. Our species began its evolution in the star cluster Pleiades in the constellation Taurus more than two million years ago. It became apparent we were on a path of using up the natural resources of the two planets we occupied. Almost 500,000 years ago, we explored and settled our most dominant planet within the Orion constellation.

Additionally, we set up a communication station on a somewhat desolate star, the size of Earth's moon, within the constellation Canis Major. From there we claimed one more planet within Canis Minor. However, since our first visit to Earth, our explorers have gone in a myriad of directions to investigate neighboring constellations. This was out of necessity rather than curiosity."

Now captivated, Dr. Martin and Mary sit stunned at this unbelievable story, while Daniel proceeds with his tale as if onboard a spacecraft speaking to an alien.

Daniel interrupts and recites from memory, "Amos 5:8 ~ Seek him that maketh the seven stars and Orion; and turneth the shadow of death into the morning and maketh the day dark with night; that calleth for the waters of the sea and poureth them out upon the face of the Earth; The Lord is his name. Job 38:31 ~ canst thou bind the sweet influences of Pleiades, or loose the bands of Orion?"

The alien interjects, *"Our journey, man's journey, has been transcribed throughout all written history, by our species and yours. Much of what I am about to share has been a part of your society, Earth's society since new-man's creation.*

As we claimed each new planet, it became necessary to build space barges to deliver supplies from one to another. In addition, realizing the need to transport our people between the star systems, we constructed massive crafts, built entirely in the confines of space. Due to the amount of time it takes to go from one star system to another, each ship was designed to house self-sufficient cities. All of our motherships house small modules to transport our people back and forth between those ships to the surfaces of the planets we inhabit and explore.

We constructed satellites in space and on multiple stars, along our journey, in order to institute interstellar communication. Often, though elaborate, that system does fail us due to the position of the stars, cosmic dust storms, and debris."

Daniel's mind is boggled. "So what led you here to us, to Earth?"

"Every twenty-six thousand years there is a Galactic

Alignment within the Milky Way."

"A kind of galactic roadmap, or highway."

"Yes that is a good analogy. During one of those alignments, 200,000 years ago, having depleted the resources of our other planets, the seven transportation ships were deployed to explore your solar system. Amidst that visit, we discovered two planets worth further study: Earth and Mars. Finding one planet was more than we could have hoped for, finding two was astonishing. At that time, Earth had one huge continent completely surrounded by water."

"Pangaea."

"Correct." The alien agrees. *"Earth's atmosphere offered an ideal environment for our survival. It has an atmosphere nearly identical to the birthplace of our existence. This discovery was a pleasant anomaly. No other planet we had discovered, or settled, had ever offered a duplicate atmosphere. Without hesitation, we began to build a series of communication towers that you call pyramids, on your planet. However, Earth, at that time, was primitive. Dinosaurs roamed Earth, along with many of the mammals that still exist today. Many of the lifeforms we encountered on your planet were unlike any we had ever encountered before."*

Daniel interrupts the alien. "Dinosaurs? That is impossible. Dinosaurs became extinct sixty-five million years ago."

"True, with the exception of a sub-species from the Cretaceous period that managed to survive and re-populate the Earth. We lost two of our great explorers to those predators. Therefore, we determined that your world was too hostile to inhabit, at that time."

"Didn't you have weapons to defend yourselves

from those creatures?"

"We had weapons, but often our explorers became victims to the element of surprise."

"You mentioned Mars."

"Yes. Although half the size of Earth, Mars was nearly as lush, and with a similar atmosphere, even though the geomagnetic field surrounding Mars was not as great as your world. Nonetheless, it was void of any life form that could threaten our existence. Therefore, we chose Mars, over Earth, as the first planet to colonize within your solar system. As with Earth, we sent hovercrafts to the surface of Mars to test the environment. Our team determined it to be inhabitable.

Having spent considerable time exploring Earth before Mars, time was running out before the Galactic Alignment shifted. If we did not leave your solar system soon, we would not have another window to leave your galaxy for another 26,000 years. In an effort to speed the process of discovery, we decided to land one of our cities on Mars. Built in the confines of space, this would be the first time that one of our massive crafts would attempt to land on a planet's surface. Unfortunately, we miscalculated the ship's entry into the Mars atmosphere. The ship malfunctioned as it descended toward the planet and plummeted to its surface."

"How is that possible? With all of the technology I see aboard this ship, how could you have made such a mistake?"

"Understand we were explorers, scientists, seeking refuge thousands of years ago, without direction. Our space technology, though much more sophisticated than that of Earth's today, was not without flaws. As the mothership fell helplessly through the atmosphere of Mars, it broke apart.

Each piece, upon hitting the Mars surface, generated force greater than a twenty-megaton bomb. This caused an extreme polar shift, and fallout from the blast destroyed the entire face of the planet."

"What became of the explorers who were on that ship?"

"Mars became shrouded in a cloud of radioactive dust and debris. We could not risk more lives. We had no choice but to abandon the thousands of souls onboard that vessel. With no other options, the remaining six cities returned to further explore Earth.

Although time was of the essence, we could not risk an attempt to land another ship, so we sent hovercrafts to Earth to gather as much information as possible. Once we had completed our studies, we the counsel, made the decision, despite the dangers, to leave a team of scientists to set up and build colonies on Earth while awaiting our return."

"Was this your first encounter with man?"

"Earth's man did not exist at that time, at least not in the form that you are familiar with. The team we left behind conducted a series of experiments with the various species of mammals, mainly the primates, while the remaining six motherships returned to our worlds to share what the crews aboard them had discovered."

"I'm curious, how are you able to travel such distances? What is the main source of energy used to operate your ships?"

"Over time, we harnessed and learned to use several types of energy. It was several thousand years before we transformed our ships and mastered the use of fusion energy. Since then, we have incorporated Orgone energy as a means for curing the ill

and calming the mind, thus enhancing the wellbeing of man. Over time, we have learned how to alter light and sound as a mechanism for every imaginable use, from killing harmful bacteria to manipulating and moving solid mass."

"What was the reaction when your six ships reached your worlds and you told them about Earth?"

"The rejoining of our past civilization was not what we had expected. Not unlike the dilemma you may face in the near future, the people of our worlds had depleted most of the natural resources on all of our planets. As I mentioned, we built our ships to seek out more planets within our star system in order to sustain life. We knew this day would come. Finding worlds with an atmosphere, and the elements conducive to our existence is a daunting task. Furthermore, early on, we discovered that the effect of entering a planet's atmosphere accelerates the aging process. Unfortunately, each time we left our worlds, and then returned, generations had vanished, both on our occupied planets and for those left to colonize Earth. In essence we became time travelers."

"Einstein's Theory of Relativity. Though time never stops, time slows for any object that moves at a great speed."

"You are correct."

"Was Einstein one of you?"

"Einstein, Da Vinci, Tesla, Newton, Sklodowska, Faraday, Archimedes, Aristotle, all, like many of the great and knowledgeable among you, past and present, are souls of the Gods."

The alien hesitates for a moment as if thinking, or perhaps feeling faint.

Uncertain of his demeanor, Daniel says, "Please continue."

The alien regains his composure. *"Our last exploration proved to be the most devastating. After leaving Earth and rendezvousing with our worlds, we discovered that two of our planets had completely depleted all of their natural resources. Wandering souls, androids, and mutant shells were all that remained. Our third and fourth planets had nearly depleted all of their resources as well. This was not the only challenge's we had to face. For those of us onboard the exploration ships, the repercussions of living in space had created an irreversible metamorphosis. Though minor in the beginning, these changes to our bodies would come to alter the course of all humankind. Prior to our returning to Earth, and before their physical demise, the governing Elders of all our planets had scribed a journal, a diary of sorts. It depicted the self-annihilation of humankind, and offered advice to those that may survive. This would become the book upon which we would build a new world."*

"The Bible?"

"The Book of Knowledge, the basis for all religion."

With his eyes closed, Daniel wipes his forehead as though he may pass out, and then continues with the conversation with himself. Mary and Dr. Martin take notice of Daniels actions as he lies on the sofa, and try to follow what he is talking about without interruption.

"Are you okay?" Daniel questions.

"Yes, I'll be fine." The alien hesitates, as if to regain his equanimity, and then begins the conversation again. *"Realizing the urgency to save our*

species, we gathered as many of the remaining life forms as possible onto our ships with the intent to relocate them to your world. At that time, each of our motherships could only house ten thousand physical beings. Eventually, we altered our crafts to house twenty thousand, such as the ship you see before you."

"Why would you not have taken the wandering souls with you?"

"We took as many as possible. Unfortunately, outside of the human body, or shell, the soul is a strong energy force, and though the soul does not take up defined space, it does alter kinetic energy. The combined energy of the billions of souls from our world would have overwhelmed the mechanics of our ships, even when encased in crystal; a substance we found somewhat useful for housing the soul until finding a host."

"How is crystal useful in housing a soul?"

"Crystal decreases the effect of the energy the soul discharges while encased within."

"In other words, you transport the soul in crystal to the host, or shell, you intend for it to inhabit."

"Not always, but often."

"That helps to explain the mystery surrounding the Crystal Skulls."

"This new dilemma left us wondering what would happen to those entities we had to leave behind. We had never dealt with a situation like this before, so we had no way of knowing with certainty that the soul could survive without a shell, indefinitely. The emotion we had to endure from this departure was all-consuming. We left behind souls that had sustained throughout all of our known time, as fathers, mothers, brothers, and sisters, now on desolate rocks, once known as the planets we called home. This was the most heart-wrenching *departure our species would ever have to endure."*

Daniel's face exudes the eternal pain and heartache of the alien. "I am sorry for your people."

"I know. We must stop for now. I have grown tired. Rest my son. We will talk further in a while."

Daniel's vision of the alien fades. He drops his chin to his chest. Then, ever so slightly, he gently lifts his head off the pillow, and with his fingers spread, he stretches his arms slowly, as if reaching toward the heavens. Without opening them, a tear falls from each eye. Suddenly, he slumps back on the sofa and rests quietly.

Mary realizes the conversation is over. "Daniel, I'm going to count to three. When I count to three, you will awaken. Do you understand?"

"Yes."

"One. Two. Three."

In an instant the wind outside subsides, and the aura surrounding Daniel's body disappears.

Daniel appears groggy, and Mary offers him a glass of water, but he rejects it. "I'm fine. I'm just going to lie here for a moment."

"Sure."

While Daniel lies on the sofa, Dr. Martin and Mary step into her front office, closing the door behind them. Mary sits at her desk and Dr. Martin in a chair across from her.

"What do you make of today's session, Dr. Martin?"

"Well, my dear, I believe Daniel has an unusual imagination."

"So, are you discounting everything he said in there?" Mary points to the door of her session room.

"Well, of course."

Dr. Martin observes Mary's face. "I hope you are not buying into this fantastic adventure he is taking us on. Are you?"

Mary slowly shakes her head. "No, Dr. Martin. But you must admit his story seemed to be very well put together."

Despite her denial, Dr. Martin doubts her sincerity and believes Mary is starting to consider Daniel's tale of abduction.

The doctor becomes both apprehensive and concerned. "How so, my dear?"

"I don't know. Maybe it's the way he described the aliens' situation. I mean, Daniel did offer an interesting theory as to how Mars may have once been inhabitable. In theory, if Mars was the victim of the massive impact from the falling pieces of the ship that broke apart, as Daniel described, it would have destroyed everything on the planet. Radiation from the fallout would have changed the entire landscape. After all, scientists have determined that at one time, it is probable life did exist on Mars."

"What are you doing, my dear?"

"What do you mean?"

"I mean, what are you doing? Why are you trying to substantiate his story? I hope you realize that Daniel's tale is just that, an illusion of what he hopes to be true."

Mary considers Dr. Martin's words, "I know you

are right. I think my imagination is running away with me. Let's forget I even brought it up."

9:15 p.m.

Aboard the shuttle, on their way to the Las Vegas airstrip, Mary and Daniel do not speak, acting as if they are strangers.

Finally, as Daniel drives them toward her house, he cannot contain himself any longer. "Well, come on, out with it, woman. Let's hear all the details of my dementia."

"Daniel, you are not crazy." Mary takes time to gather her thoughts. "It's just ... well ... you are ... your mind is apparently playing out some kind of charade, a game to validate your past experience with your grandmother. Or it's possible you are trying to justify your years of hard work with the agency."

"I don't understand."

"I know." Mary thinks aloud. "Why didn't you tell me about her?"

"Who?"

"I understand, from Dr. Martin, that you were close to your mother's mom."

"So, is this subjective reasoning?"

"Not exactly."

"I'm afraid to ask what you mean by that." Daniel taps his fingers on the steering wheel.

"We did, or actually, Dr. Martin conducted an in-depth background profile on you and your family."

"Now what, you and Dr. Martin are playing detective? You haven't involved my family in any of this, have you? You'll scare the hell out of them."

"No, Daniel, they were simply told that we were conducting a routine investigation."

"So, should I thank you for not telling them that I'm losing my mind?"

"Daniel, you are not losing your mind. You said a few things under hypnosis which led us to believe you were close to your grandmother. We thought, perhaps, if we could determine to what degree of closeness you had with her, we might be able to define the tricks your subconscious is playing on you."

"I hope you're not going to tell me this is getting sick and perverted."

"No. Not at all," Mary answers. "As you know, the subconscious is far more intelligent than the conscious. It would appear your subconscious has taken the relationship you had with your grandmother, your acquired knowledge, and the work you are doing on the Terrestrials Project, and manifested it into an illusion of who man is and where man came from." Mary waits for Daniel to respond, but he does not. She breaks the silence. "What? No comment?"

"What can I say? I guess I would have to review the session tapes to understand exactly what you are hinting at."

"Daniel, I'm not hinting at anything."

"So, when can I see the videos, or at least read

the transcripts?"

"I'm not sure."

"Why is that?"

"Look Daniel, I don't think it would be wise for you to see the videos or read the transcripts until we have finished our analysis."

Daniel focuses his eyes on the road ahead. "And when will that be?"

"I don't know."

"Well, I would like to see them."

"Well, you can't."

"Well, why not?"

"Daniel, besides the fact that you are annoying me, you sound like a five-year-old."

Mary becomes quiet as she looks out her window at the desert. In the distance, she sees a series of lights similar to those seen the night before. Daniel glances at Mary and discovers what has attracted her attention.

Out of the blue, he remarks, "It's them again."

"Them who?"

"I don't know. I don't even know why I said that." He steers the car off to the side of the road and stops.

"No, Daniel, don't pull over."

"But, Mary, it's the same lights ..."

Mary interrupts him and shouts, as if frightened by what she sees, "Daniel, don't pull over!"

Daniel drives back onto the highway and continues on his way. Upon passing the same mound as the night before, the lights in the distance vanish.

Mary regains her composure. "You see, it was nothing. It must have been a reflection, just as Dr. Martin suggested."

"You told Dr. Martin about last night?"

"I had to."

"You had to?"

"Daniel, I can't explain it to you now."

He exclaims, "Well, from where I sit, now would be the perfect time."

Suddenly, a light appears in her side-view mirror, as it did the previous night. With anxiety setting in, Mary glances in the mirror. She does not turn to look out the rear window for fear that if she does the light will disappear.

Her eyes are transfixed on the mirror. "Nothing makes sense lately."

"What do you mean?"

Mary does not answer as she focuses on the disturbance in the sky. The light is now a constant. She tries to reason in her mind that it could be a reflection. However, intuition tells her it is not.

"Daniel, how fast are you going?"

Daniel knows he is not speeding. "What?"

"Daniel, speed up." Mary continues to focus on the light in the mirror.

"Why?"

She is now anxious. "Just go faster!"

He floors it.

The light remains constant in her mirror, despite the various mountains they pass, which tells her it is not a reflection.

Daniel adjusts his rearview mirror and discovers the same light.

"What the hell is it?"

Mary shouts, "Slow down."

"Are you serious?"

"Slow down!"

Daniel slows the vehicle, and in an instant, the light disappears.

He glances back into the rearview mirror but sees nothing. "What do you think it was?"

Mary thinks before speaking, and does her best to throw Daniel off her true summation. "It must have been a reflection from the stars bouncing off the back of the car."

"Mary, I have never seen a reflection ..."

Frightened at what Daniel is about to say, Mary exclaims, "Daniel, please!"

"Babe, are you all right?" He is concerned for Mary's mental well-being.

Without notice, the headlights of the car shine on a tiger standing in the middle of the road. Daniel swerves to avoid hitting it. He drives the car off on the shoulder and stops. At that instant, a solid black object passes quickly overhead, creating a gust of wind strong enough to rock the car. It's so big it blocks out the stars before ascending into the night sky. Within seconds, it vanishes out of sight. When they peer back at the road, the tiger is gone.

Daniel is perplexed. "Where did it go?"

Confounded, Mary states, "I don't know. Let's go home."

Fifteen minutes pass. Daniel turns into Mary's driveway and parks the car. He opens his door and then walks around to open her car door.

Mary gets out, and Daniel escorts her to the front door. A breeze begins to stir. Something seems to be rustling in the bushes that border Mary's property. Daniel gazes around, but sees nothing. Nonetheless, his eyes are transfixed on the bushes.

Mary notices his trance-like state. "Daniel, what is it?" When he does not answer, she becomes uneasy. She strains to see what has captured his attention. All she sees is the breeze rustling the leaves of the shrub.

"Daniel, are you okay?"

He snaps back to reality. "Yes, I'm fine. Come on, let's go in."

Mary unlocks the door to the house, and they enter. Off in the distance, the lights from the city flicker as he closes the door behind them. Mary turns on a light. For a moment, they both just stand looking into each other's eyes.

Daniel leans forward and kisses her. "Would you like for me to stay tonight?"

Mary feels uneasy. "Yes, that would be great."

Then, out of nowhere, a primordial amorous feeling comes over them. They embrace, and begin to act like young lovers who can't keep their hands off of each other. Kissing passionately, they disrobe, leaving a trail of clothes as they make their way to the bedroom. Once in the room, Daniel makes passionate love to Mary, as if it were their last day on Earth.

Shutters in the window filter streams of silvery light as the rising moon shines into the darkened bedroom. The bright moonlight casts the faint outline of a shadowy figure brushing by the window. Daniel notices the passing shadow and stops kissing Mary, who lies on top of him.

Daniel, now wide-eyed and alert, "Did you see that?"

Mary turns her head. "See what?"

The wind has kicked up a notch outside as they continue with their lovemaking. Something scrapes by the window, and Daniel is compelled to look again. Although he sees nothing, Mary stops to see what has his attention.

Daniel begins kissing Mary's neck. "It must have been a tree branch." He then rolls Mary onto her back and caresses her. Finally satisfied, after another hour of lustful lovemaking, Daniel positions Mary on her side. With an unusual burst of energy, he climbs out of bed and pops her on the bare butt with the back of his hand.

Mary rubs her butt cheek and hollers, "Ouch!"

Daniel wraps a blanket around his waist. "I'm going to get a drink. Would you like something?"

Physically and emotionally drained, Mary remarks, "No, thanks, you've done plenty for me already. I'm going to take a shower."

As Mary climbs out of bed, Daniel playfully grabs her arm and pulls her near, planting a big, wet kiss on her lips.

Annoyed with the slobber, Mary wipes her mouth with the back of her hand. "Have you been taking Viagra?"

"Nope." He rubs his nose against hers while giggling. "I don't need Viagra. It's all natural, Baby. It's all me."

Mary shakes her head.

"Don't go anywhere. I'll be right back, Baby." Daniel kisses her again and heads off to the kitchen.

A shadowy figure passes by the shuttered bedroom window as Mary saunters into the bathroom. Outside the bathroom window, Mary glimpses an unexplained movement. She pulls back the shade and peers out. She sees nothing. Then a breeze causes the cypress tree beside the window to sway, allowing the moonlight to reflect off the face of what she perceives to be an alien being staring back at her. Mary screams and backs away.

Startled, Daniel runs into the bathroom from the kitchen.

"Honey, what is it? What's wrong?"

Trembling, Mary points to the window. "There's something out there."

Daniel hurries to the window and opens the shade. The only thing he sees is the cypress tree dancing in the wind.

Mary cautiously walks to the window and looks out, but nothing is there.

She's baffled, "I'm telling you, I saw something!"

Daniel takes her in his arms, strokes her hair, and kisses her forehead. "All right, Baby, I believe you. Calm down, I'm right here. You go ahead and take your shower, and I'll scout around outside."

"I'll wait."

Daniel, recognizing her resolute tone, returns to the bedroom and quickly slips on some clothes. He grabs his gun from its holster, making sure it is loaded, then tucks it into the waistband of his pants. Stepping carefully out the front door, Daniel walks to the side of the house, scanning the bushes as he passes. He stops just below the bathroom window. He looks up and realizes the window is more than six feet off the ground.

He sees nothing in the immediate area, except for the cypress tree, alongside the house, continuing to sway back and forth in the breeze. After another quick glance around, he goes back inside.

In the bathroom, Mary stands with her hands to her face, still trembling. He moves past her and up to the window, pushes the shade open and peers out once again.

"Honey, nothing is out there. You would have to be at least seven feet tall to look through this window."

"I'm telling you, something was out there."

"I'm sure there was." Daniel approaches Mary and attempts to pull her close into the comfort of his arms.

Mary pushes him away, shouting, "Don't patronize me."

Realizing her manic state, Daniel fights to wrap his arms around her. "Mary, calm down. I believe you. Why don't you take a nice hot shower and relax? I'll be right here. I'm going into the kitchen to make us something warm to drink."

"Okay, Okay." Mary steadies herself enough to take a shower. "Please, don't go too far."

She turns the shower on and climbs in while Daniel moves toward the door.

He reassures her before leaving. "I'll be right down the hall if you need me."

Mary positions the shower curtain in place. "Okay. I'm fine, now."

Daniel goes into the hall, but leaves the bathroom door open.

While Mary is in the shower, she gets an uneasy feeling that someone may be watching her. Cautiously, she pulls the shower curtain open enough to peek through, and sees the shadowy figure outside the bathroom window. Though scared, Mary's curiosity prods her to step out of the shower. Facing her fears, she hastily pushes the shade open. In an instant, the unrecognizable being in the window disappears. Bravely, she closes the shade.

Feeling a little more secure, she returns to the shower and finishes. After turning off the water, she grabs a towel from the rack and begins to dry off. Once dry, she wraps the towel around her hair and draws back the shower curtain. The sudden appearance of Daniel, standing before her like a statue, holding a cup of hot cocoa in each hand, startles her.

"Daniel!"

Her scream is unsettling, and he spills hot chocolate on the floor while trying to keep from getting the hot liquid all over him.

Mary retorts, "You scared the hell out of me!"

"You scared the hell out of me. I thought you could use something warm to drink."

In a confused and frightened state, Mary stands before him stark naked, except for the towel turbaned in her hair. She throws her arms around Daniel's neck and sobs against his chest.

Bewildered, Daniel stands with a cup in each hand as Mary hangs onto his neck.

She collects herself with an effort. "What is happening to us?"

CHAPTER 6
His Name Is God

Daniel and Mary spend the weekend together at her place. Having plenty of provisions, they never leave the house. Each night together offers a repeat performance of the night before - a light breeze in the air, strange shadows outside the windows, and Daniel's insatiable lust for making love.

MONDAY - 6:30 a.m.

After a restless night's sleep, Daniel drives while a physically and mentally exhausted Mary looks out the window in silence. It is a calm spring morning in the Nevada desert. The sun peeks out from behind the mountains in the background. On their way to the airstrip, Mary notices the mound they encountered with the dancing lights.

Tired and bewildered, she makes a request, "Daniel, I need you to pull over, please."

"Okay." Wondering why the request, He steers the car to the side of the road and parks. "Are you all right?"

"Yes, I'm fine. I just want to check something." Mary gets out of the car.

Daniel glances out the passenger window in her direction and notices she is walking toward the small hill.

Aloud he says, "What is she doing?"

He jumps from the car and follows as she approaches the mound.

Daniel is curious, and hurries to catch up with her. "What are we doing?"

"Exploring."

"What exactly are you exploring?"

Ignoring his question, Mary stops and observes her surroundings. She mumbles, "No tracks, no flashlight, no nothing."

Concerned about her frame of mind, he asks again, "Mary, what are you doing?"

She does not answer and stays focused on the mound as she moves toward it. Daniel follows close by, trying to discern what she is looking for.

As they approach, the rising sun and fresh air renews Mary's intuitive nature. "Something doesn't make sense."

"How's that?"

"Where did the tiger come from? Better yet, where did it go?"

Jokingly, he responds, "Home."

"Funny, Daniel, funny." They keep walking toward the mound. Mary veers to one side of it, and Daniel follows.

Mary stops, then points. "This is where I saw a flicker of light from the flashlight as it entered the cave."

"The flashlight entered the cave. Now there's a feat." Daniel chuckles.

Mary glares at him. "You know what I mean."

They continue to scout around, but there is no sign of an entrance.

"How can you be sure it was a cave?"

"Daniel, I know what I saw. You saw it too."

"I don't dispute seeing a tiger, Mary, but I didn't see a light go into any cave. Come on, it was pitch-black. The desert can play tricks on you just as much at night as it can during the day. We both know that."

Mary is emphatic. "I know what I saw."

Daniel stares at her.

"Don't look at me that way! You know that we both could not have imagined the same thing."

Daniel tries to remains calm. "You seem to have seen more than I did."

"What does that mean? Do you think I was hallucinating? Is that what you're implying?"

"No, Baby, but be realistic. I'm pointing out it was dark, and we were frightened by the animal running ..."

Mary cuts him off. "You mean the tiger!"

"Okay, the tiger. It all happened so fast, how can we be sure of what we saw?"

"I thought you believed?" Mary is frustrated.

"Believed what? Are you talking about UFO's?"

Contemplating her next words carefully, Mary realizes that she cannot discuss any part of Daniel's sessions, for fear of disrupting the process of unraveling his story under hypnosis. "Come on, or we'll be late. Perhaps I *am* overreacting."

AREA 51 - 9:45 a.m.

Mary and Daniel amble down the hall toward the office.

"Did the chief say what he wanted?" Daniel asks.

Mary responds with an unusually stiff and composed attitude. "Not really. Just that he had some follow-up information for us."

They approach the door to the chief's outer office. Daniel turns the handle and pushes the door open.

"Follow up to what?" he asks, curiously.

"I don't know, but we're about to find out,"

Upon entering, Daniel greets Chief Rankin's secretary, "Hello, Jean."

She nods toward each of them, "Good morning, Agent Scudder, Agent Drake. You may go in. The chief is waiting."

They enter the office to the chief of The Terrestrial Project. He is sitting behind a highly polished mahogany desk with his hands folded around a mug of black coffee.

Daniel speaks first. "Good morning, Sir."

"Good morning, Agent Scudder, Agent Drake." He points to the chairs in front of his desk. "Have a seat."

While Daniel and Mary sit, the chief opens one of the drawers. He pulls out a flashlight, and walks to the front of his desk.

He leans against the desk. "Here, I believe this belongs to you."

He hands Daniel the flashlight.

Daniel reaches for the light. "Where did you get this?"

"Well, after reading both of your reports on the incident in the desert, I did some investigating. It seems that a tiger escaped from its cage at the Anderson Ranch earlier that day. It returned home the following morning. The tiger's trainer found your flashlight inside its cage."

Puzzled, Mary questions, "Inside the cage?"

"That's right. Apparently, the tiger came home and crawled back into the cage on its own."

Mary finds his explanation somewhat shallow. "Don't you find that a bit unusual? I mean, come on, Chief, this tiger carries the flashlight home with him, then takes it inside his cage? Isn't that a bit far-fetched?"

"No, not really. According to the trainer, that particular cat has lived in the same cage its entire life. It probably just went back home. And, I suppose, the tiger most likely considered the flashlight a toy."

"How do you explain the fact that we saw the tiger again on Friday night?"

"I don't know. Maybe it wandered off for a second time?"

"What about the lights?"

"What lights? Are you talking about the flashlight?" the chief asks.

"I'm talking about the lights that we saw off in the distance and above us as Agent Scudder and I drove down the highway."

"Oh, I don't know, Agent Drake. What do you think? Isn't it possible that you experienced an illusion created by the reflection of the moon and the stars?"

Daniel chimes in. "That's what I said."

Mary glares at Daniel. "You know what we both saw!"

Chief Rankin detects the hostility in Mary's voice. "Drake, is this situation with Scudder starting to overwhelm you? If it is, I can have Dr. Martin take over."

Fearing that she might lose control of the sessions, Mary replies, "No, no, Chief, not at all. You know, you're right, perhaps I am overreacting."

"Now that's the Drake I'm used to. Please understand I take this incident seriously. However, everything did seem to check out. Nevertheless, should you encounter another episode like this in the future; I do want to hear about it. Now, if you have nothing further to discuss, you are dismissed."

Daniel and Mary look at each other.

Reading Mary's face, Daniel answers for both of them, "I think you have solved the mystery."

"Good. I am here to help in any way I can."

Having said his piece, Chief Rankin returns to his chair and picks up his cup of coffee.

Daniel flicks the flashlight on and off as he and Mary leave. The chief watches them exit, and then reaches for his phone.

In the reception area, Daniel and Mary bid good-bye to Jean.

Daniel tries for a lighthearted tone as they walk toward Mary's office. "Well, that answers a lot of questions."

Remaining unresponsive, Mary quickens her pace. Upon reaching her office, she hurries to her desk and opens her laptop.

"What are you doing?"

While searching the web for a map, Mary replies in a firm voice, "Just a minute, you'll see." She pulls up a map of the mountain range and valley between her home and Anderson Ranch. "I'm almost finished with my calculations." Finally, Mary points to the map. "Look right here. This is where the Anderson Ranch is located."

Daniel leans in and focuses where her fingertip is touching the map. "And your point is?"

"My point is the Anderson Ranch is here." She moves her finger across the computer screen. "And this is where we encountered the tiger."

"So?"

"So?" Mary shows Daniel the calculations on the screen. "The Anderson Ranch is more than thirty miles away, on the other side of the valley."

"What are you suggesting?"

"How did the tiger get there, to that part of the desert?"

"I don't know," Daniel half-heartedly answers, "I suppose it walked."

"Let me point out that not once, but twice we saw the tiger in that exact location, within two days. Not to mention that it carried a flashlight all the way home in its mouth, across the mountain and through the Las Vegas valley."

"So where else would he carry it, in his pocket?"

Failing to find the humor in Daniel's comment, Mary glares at him.

"Okay, I know. Not funny. But, listen to reason. I thought the way the chief explained how the tiger got there to be plausible. And, maybe it did consider the flashlight a toy."

"How do you explain the distance the cat had to travel at night?"

Daniel does his best to allay Mary's worries. "Look, it's a tiger, a nocturnal, muscular animal, quite capable of traveling that distance."

"How do you answer for what we saw as we were leaving the desert?"

"As for the lights in the car mirrors, and the dark object we thought took off from the mound, I surmise we experienced an illusion. I believe the lights were merely reflections. It was so dark we really couldn't see anything clearly. As for the gust of wind, it's the desert. Dust devils are prevalent, day or night." Daniel hesitates, "I thought that you were the skeptic here."

"And I thought you were the believer."

Annoyed by her reference, Daniel throws his hands up in the air. "Believer in what?" He analyzes Mary's face and realizes to what she is referring. "You really do think we encountered extraterrestrials, don't you?"

With exaggerated moves, Mary turns off the laptop and closes it. "I'm not sure what I believe anymore."

1:00 p.m.

Mary enters Dr. Martin's office. A video of Daniel's last session plays on a television screen. Dr. Martin stands in front of the monitor speaking to several of his colleagues.

She approaches Dr. Martin. "What is going on here?"

Dr. Martin does not hesitate. "I invited a few of my colleagues to observe Agent Scudder's last session."

Mary stands mute, then stares at him with hands on her hips.

He feels the need to offer further explanation. "Of course, they are here as part of a concerted effort to determine the underlying motive behind Agent Scudder's delusion."

"Of course." Mary rolls her eyes. "Dr. Martin, may I speak with you in private?"

"Certainly, my dear," Dr. Martin agrees cheerfully, oblivious to her seething anger.

He turns to his colleagues. "Gentlemen, please excuse me for one moment while I confer with Agent Drake."

Mary and Dr. Martin take a few steps away from his colleagues and begin to quietly converse.

"Dr. Martin, I'm not so sure that you should be doing this."

"Doing what, my dear?"

Mary does not buy into his act of innocence. "I believe that we should keep this to ourselves until we have evaluated each session carefully."

"But, my dear, may I ask why?"

"We have no idea what motivated Daniel's delusion or what it might lead to. We don't even know when these sessions will conclude."

"Agent Drake, I think that your attachment to Daniel is overshadowing the merit of this discovery."

"Discovery of what?"

"Of the ability, my dear, for the subconscious mind to manifest the improbable, through abstract theory, into possibility."

Mary becomes more annoyed and snaps at him. "What the hell are you talking about? Dr. Martin, you are turning this investigation into a spectacle, and I won't have it!"

Dr. Martin motions for Mary to lower her voice, as he glances toward his colleagues.

"All I'm suggesting, Drake," he moves closer and whispers as though it might be a secret, "is that Scudder has taken his life's work of trying to prove the existence of extraterrestrials and turned it into plausibility."

"So, you do believe what he is saying?"

Dr. Martin takes a step backwards away from her, and replies in a normal voice, "Not a word." Mary is confused as the doctor continues. "I'm not certain, but I believe, as these sessions progress, you will find Daniel is taking his accumulated knowledge of possible abductions, his knowledge of science and theology, and combining it with evolutionary theories. I conclude, and so do many of the others in this room, he is doing all of this to justify his personal desire to prove the existence of extraterrestrials."

"I'm not quite ready to believe your theory. However, assuming there is some validity to your conclusion, why are all of these people here? How can they possibly assist with these sessions?"

"Assist? They are not here to assist, my dear. They are here to observe the power of what can happen when the subconscious is coupled with an exceptionally intellectual mind."

"So now Daniel is a sideshow?"

"Well, I wouldn't call it that."

"Oh, no? Well, I would. I no longer need your help. Agent Scudder is a closed case study to you. I'll be continuing the sessions alone."

"Young lady ..."

Before Dr. Martin can say another word, Mary storms from the room. She returns to her office to make a few notes before her next session with Daniel.

3:50 p.m.

Mary is adjusting the camcorder as Daniel enters the session room, holding his nose with a bloodstained tissue. "Hi, Babe."

She hastens to finish what she is doing and hurries toward Daniel to examine him. "Are you all right?" She reaches for a fresh tissue from the end table.

"Yes, I'll be fine." He tilts his head back while Mary dabs his nose. "Apparently, Dr. Martin ordered the removal of something from my nose. At least, that is what I assume."

She stops dabbing. "Actually, I did."

Daniel grabs the tissue from Mary's hand and pushes her away. "I would like to know what the hell is going on? Chief Rankin took me off all case studies until you finish with these sessions. What is happening, Mary? What am I telling you under hypnosis? And please, don't tell me nothing important."

The chief knocks at the door to Mary's outer office, and then opens it and walks in.

"Drake, can I see you, please?"

"Yes, sir. Give me a moment."

Chief Rankin waits in the outer office while Mary directs Daniel to the sofa. She gives him a few more tissues "Here. Keep your head back and don't move. I'll be right back."

Mary walks into the outer office, closing the door to the session room. She notices that the chief has left the door leading into the hallway ajar.

"Yes, Chief?"

"I understand you informed Dr. Martin that he would no longer be needed for Agent Scudder's sessions?"

"That is correct."

"Drake, you can't do that."

"And why not? I'm the one who invited him to be a part of these sessions with Daniel in the first place."

"Yes, but Daniel's case has become so complicated, I've deem it necessary for Dr. Martin to be present during Daniel's regressive state."

"Well, I disagree."

"Then I'm ordering you to allow Dr. Martin to be present during each session." He moves toward the door and pushes it open. "Dr. Martin, would you come in, please?"

Dr. Martin steps through the doorway. Sheepishly, he tries to explain his point of view to Mary. "My dear, I'm sorry it has to come to this, but you have to understand, Agent Scudder is a unique case study."

Angered by this decision, Mary goes to her desk, sits, and stares venomously at the chief. "I'm off the case."

"No, you are not."

"I want nothing else to do with this ... this farce Dr. Martin is creating."

"Regardless of whether you consider it a farce or not, you will remain on this case. Dr. Martin feels you are the only person that Agent Scudder will open up to, at least in the manner of his past regressions." He turns to address the doctor. "I'm sorry Dr. Martin, will you excuse us for a moment, please? I need to have a private word with Agent Drake."

"Certainly." The doctor steps into the hallway.

The chief moves a few papers from the corner of Mary's desk and sits. He looks at her earnestly. "I realize how all of this must be getting to you, but we need to get to the bottom of Daniel's problem."

"Daniel doesn't have a problem."

"Not on the surface, maybe, but the underlying implications of these sessions represent a bigger picture. For fourteen years, Daniel has done his best to prove that extraterrestrials exist, and to no avail. Then, out of nowhere, he doesn't show up for work one day. Come on, that isn't like him. In addition, he's developed nosebleeds."

"Chief, you know his nosebleed is caused by the object I ordered removed from his left nostril."

"That's today, but what about this past week?" He pauses for a minute. "I believe Daniel wants, no needs, for aliens to exist. And that need has taken control of his subconscious."

"And where did you hear that? From Dr. Martin, no doubt."

Chief Rankin leans toward her. "Mary, I'm serious. Please, listen to me. I am perfectly aware of how close you and Daniel are. I saw it coming the first time the two of you met. I should have put an end to it then, before you became involved. Instead, I allowed the rules to be broken. I turned my head because I knew you two were perfect for this project. Don't let me down now."

"How interesting that you discovered our mutual attraction twelve years before we did."

Chief Rankin stares back without saying a word.

Mary becomes frightened by his stare and his towering closeness. She tries to change the subject. "In any case, I understand Agent Scudder has been relieved of all of his responsibilities."

The chief leans back. "He has been placed on temporary leave, with pay, just until we have completed all necessary sessions. So, when do you expect this will come to a conclusion?"

"I'm not sure. There is really have no way of knowing."

The chief stands. "Then I suggest we get busy. The sooner we conclude this matter, the better for us all."

He turns toward the open door. "Dr. Martin, you can come in now."

Dr. Martin enters the room, avoiding Mary's steely glare.

"Dr. Martin, I think Agent Drake is ready to begin." Chief Rankin glances back at Mary. "We are ready, right, Drake?"

Mary gets up and walks from behind her desk to the door of the session room, then turns and glares at Dr. Martin.

Despite her distain for the doctor, Mary controls her emotions. "I'll be inside, preparing Daniel for the next session."

Chief Rankin nods. "Thank you, Agent Drake."

Mary enters the session room, and the chief gives Dr. Martin instructions. "I want a full report on my desk, first thing in the morning."

"Yes, sir, I'll make sure the transcripts are ready, first thing."

With renewed assurance about who is in control, the doctor enters the session room, his demeanor projecting condescension toward Mary.

Daniel is already lying down. Mary is in her chair beside the sofa holding his hand.

Dr. Martin closes the door.

"Shall we get started?" Mary asks with disdain.

Dr. Martin takes his seat. "Please, let's do."

Folding his hands in his lap, he smiles with the knowledge he is in complete control.

Mary places Daniel's hand to his side and picks up the remote. She pushes the start button and places the remote on the end table.

"Monday, May 22, 4:00 p.m. Session four with Agent Daniel Scudder."

Taking the locket from the table beside her, she swings it back and forth in front of Daniel's eyes.

"Daniel, I want you to follow the locket with your eyes."

He does as instructed.

After placing him in a hypnotic trance, Mary asks, "Daniel, do you remember the light in the sky?"

He hesitates and then says, "Yes."

"Do you remember being taken aboard a spacecraft?"

"Yes."

"Daniel, the alien that you were talking to needed a rest. Do you remember?"

"Yes."

"Did you talk further?

"Yes, extensively."

"What did you talk about?"

"I asked the alien who he was, if he had a name."

"Did he answer?"

"Yes."

"What was his name?"

"His name is God."

Dr. Martin scoots to the edge of his chair and looks over at Mary to examine her reaction to Daniel's answer.

As before, an aura surrounds Daniel's body, and the wind begins to blow ferociously outside.

Mary, feels Dr. Martin's eyes upon her, but refuses to acknowledge him. Instead, she focuses her attention on Daniel and the session.

"Did you say God?" Mary asks.

"Yes. He is the one whom they call God."

"As in *the* God?"

Without interruption, Mary and Dr. Martin listen intently while Daniel speaks in alternating voices.

In his trance, Daniel is aboard the spacecraft. He continues his conversation with the alien.

"As the oldest and wisest, I was proclaimed The God of Gods, The Great Explorer, by the combined order of the Elders. It was I who first discovered your solar system over 200,000 years ago."

"How old are you?" Daniel asks.

"This shell possesses more than seventy-eight thousand Earth years. However, I have housed several since we began our exploration of Earth, and the evolution of your humankind."

"Okay," Daniel says mockingly, "and you say that your present body is seventy-eight thousand years old?"

"Yes. In Earth years, outside the confines of space, I am approximately four hundred. As you mentioned regarding the Theory of Relativity, time slows in the confines of space when traveling from one star cluster to another, our star system to yours. Our bodies age approximately one Earth year for every two hundred years in space. Though unrecognizable now, my appearance, prior to this journey, was similar to Earth's man. In space, muscle mass depletes, therefore, the body compensates. Our original shells began a physical transformation during the

first exploration to your solar system. Due to the thousands of years spent aboard these vessels, our bodies have undergone a complete metamorphosis."

"Is that why your lower extremities are so much smaller than mine?"

"Correct, and as you can see, the upper-quadrant of our shells have expanded."

"Is this the reason for the enlarged cranium and eyes?"

"Yes and no. The cranium has grown in size due to the time we have spent in space, as well as to compensate for the size of our brain. Although our eyes appear to be larger than that of Earth's man, they are not. We created a lens to help protect the retina from the effects of light in space."

Without prodding, the alien removes one of the lenses, revealing a human eye. After a moment of silence, allowing Daniel to absorb what he has seen, the alien puts the lens back in place.

"We have come to accept that no matter our exercise routine, our bodies are doomed to undergo this metamorphosis. However, in the twenty-six thousand Earth years, it took to reach home, and then to return to your world each time, our greatest detriment was the loss of our ability to procreate. The ships' higher council, the Elders, calculated the next step of our very existence, and it appeared grim. They calculated the possibility of the extinction of our physical being. Android's were created should this happen, to house our souls. To our dismay, they could not express the emotions of the human shell. We are a physical being. We need the ability to communicate in the flesh. Needless to say, we began to grow weary.

It was during this period of our history in space that we developed a way to slow the aging process even further, but this was not without risk. Upon our return to your world fifty-two thousand years ago, we experimented with a new technology, a process known as cryogenics. My shell, at the time, was the youngest and the most virile, but my knowledge was needed to lead this expedition. We could not risk the death of my physical being while in a cryogenic state. It was determined by the Elders that I should not participate.

Our intent was to use cryogenics to preserve the breeders of our world for future procreation. Unfortunately, the volunteers who offered their bodies to further our existence, died during this process. It would be several thousand years before we were able to perfect this technology. By then, I was the last breeder onboard our ships. Therefore, our scientists went to work to develop another way to preserve our species."

"And that was …"

"Artificial insemination. My seeds were frozen for future breeding; to create a new life form on Earth. Time was running out for our species of man, even though our technology was advancing rapidly. Since the colonization of man had already begun thousands of years earlier with the team of scientists that we had left behind on Earth, your world seemed the most logical place to re-populate our species. Unfortunately, before our return, the colony we had left behind had succumbed to disease, predators, and Earth's anomalies, such as earthquakes, floods, and volcanic eruptions. We returned to Earth and gathered those souls, encased them in crystal, and brought then aboard our ships.

When we first set out on our journey to explore your world, we were fertile. We had no interest in procreating with other beings. We were simply looking for new planets to inhabit, a new star to harvest for food and fuel. Then everything changed, once we could no longer breed. We needed to create new shells, new bodies to inhabit. Though Earth's primates are millions of years behind our evolutionary scale, we realized they were the last hope to sustain life in the flesh. Therefore, using this newfound technology of artificial insemination, we impregnated the various species of primates on your world with my seeds. The intervention that created Earth's man had begun. Facing certain extinction, time was of the essence. Understand, my son, you would not be here if we had not initiated this experiment."

"Now it makes sense," Daniel says, "Genesis 1:26 ~ And God said, let us make man in our image, after our likenesses.

"You must understand that the soul of man lives and grows from the human experience. The soul needs the flesh of man in order to continue."

"So it has come to pass that you need us more than we need you."

"We need each other. The Elders further calculated that unless we acted immediately, life as we knew it would end within the next thirty thousand Earth years."

"You mentioned you saw dinosaurs upon your first visit to Earth."

"That is correct."

"Are you telling me that the dinosaurs roamed Earth as recently as two hundred thousand years ago?"

"Actually, a sub-species roamed Earth as recently as fifty-two thousand years ago. Our dilemma was twofold. Not

only did we need your world to sustain life, we also needed to create a new species of man capable of housing our souls. Therefore, in order to avoid further loss of life, we decided to bring Earth's inhabitants to us.

Nearly two hundred thousand years have passed since we began our first exploration of your solar system. During this time, we have experienced the effects of gravity and kinetic energy on solid matter. With the discovery of new and better energy sources, our cities have been modified and are now capable of invading your atmosphere and landing safely. Our ships are even able to invade your oceans to harvest food and the materials necessary for us to sustain life. We have learned how to manipulate light and sound to control mass, and to protect us from human parasites and bacteria. In addition, we have conditioned our minds to communicate with the various species on Earth without vocalizing."

"You are speaking of mental telepathy; the utilization of the third eye, or Chakra."

"Yes. Communicating with nearly all the species on Earth has proven to be most valuable in maintaining ecological balance and assisting in our periodic intervention.

Realizing our dilemma, we could no longer afford to lose more shells. Due to the acceleration of age to our bodies upon entering Earth's atmosphere, each team of three explorers was limited to no more than seven days. In addition, we alternated each mission between the motherships. Eventually, we decided to bring a variety of species from your world onboard our ships for study and observation in order to limit the time spent on Earth. In essence, our six remaining ships became research centers. We quarantined sections of them to house the experiments we undertook."

"Why a variety of species?"

"We evolved from a single primate, millions of years ago, on our first planet in the star cluster Pleiades. None of the primates of Earth quite resembled that species. Our goal was to create a species of new-man to resemble the physical form of our past. It became a difficult task to determine which species of primate to inseminate. Therefore, we decided to artificially inseminate several variations of primates from your world. Having done so, we realized that the subjects of the experiments would eventually have to be returned to Earth to avoid the effects of space on the body."

Daniel interjects, "Man's missing link, Psalms 148:5-6 ~ Let them praise the name of the Lord, for he commanded and they were created. He hath also established them forever and ever; He hath made a decree which shall not pass."

Without acknowledging Daniel's comment, the alien continues, as if the remark was expected.

"The objective was to create a species of man which would resemble our past physical attributes. Each ship was assigned the responsibility of implementing and maintaining their new colony upon returning them to Earth."

Daniel chortles. "Let me guess, Norse mythology, Izanagi and Izanami, the Mayans, the Greek Gods, and so on."

"The analogy is one and the same. Let me clarify it for you. Our concern became one of sustaining life for the chosen ones. In the regions where dinosaurs existed, they were the greatest threat, often crushing or devouring the iterations of new-man. We could not allow this to happen."

"I thought you could control the various species on the Earth using mental telepathy?"

"For some unknown reason, the dinosaurs were the one exception. In addition, we were not always present. Therefore, Earth's new-man fell victim to all predators. Furthermore, the Elders had determined each experiment should remain separate in order to disseminate which race of new-man would best evolve to resemble our species of humankind – the humankind that would eventually house our souls.

Over time, these new human races on Earth became increasingly intelligent. Many of the colonies had collided, and we did not want the various races to cohabitate. We did not want them to destroy all we had worked toward in order to create a supreme species, so we needed to rethink the direction of the different colonies.

Scientists aboard our ships developed a plan to divide the one great continent and simultaneously eliminate the dinosaurs. The concept behind this plan was to displace the new species of humankind on Earth to evolve in separate, and relatively safe, environments."

Daniel concludes, "So, your exploration and the colonization of our world, upon discovering this solar system, would explain the Blombos Cave project in South Africa – the beginning of modern man. It further offers an explanation for the Paluxy River in Texas, where archeologists discovered impressions of a human's footprint with that of pre-historic dinosaurs."

"You are correct. Having completed our studies, and using hovercrafts, we brought your world to ours. We gathered the healthiest male and female life forms roaming your planet

necessary for sustaining life, as well as the most physically appealing and intellectual among new-man's colonies, and brought them aboard our ships."

"Of course," Daniel observes, "Noah's Ark."

"Philosophically, yes. Seedlings, cuttings, and roots were gathered from all forms of plant life. Once this process was complete, we positioned our mother ships in space. Having strategically calculated the pressure points of the Earth's tectonic plates, our ships simultaneously fired lasers upon the Earth's surface. The one continent that had already begun to shift prior to our intervention broke even farther apart. The ensuing volcanic eruptions that followed sent a heavy film of soot and ash into the air that surrounded your planet."

Daniel grows more excited. "'Genesis 1:6. And God said, let there be a firmament in the midst of the waters, and let it divide the waters from the waters.' This all ties in with Bernard Northrup's study on volcanism. Northrup talks about the effects the volcanic activity may have had in shaping present day Earth."

"We spent the next twenty-six thousand years in space watching over our precious cargo while the Earth heated, cooled, and thawed several times before becoming its present state."

"It's beginning to make perfect sense," Daniel becomes excited. "Carbon dating must have been altered by the effects the volcanic activity would have had on the Earth's surface. The pressure thrust upon Earth during the eruptions would have been intense, far surpassing that needed to create a man-made diamond."

"Again, you are correct. Time was our greatest enemy. It became a race to development a new species of man as quickly as possible. Although the similarities to our past shells progressed well, the challenge became at what rate would new-man's brain develop. It was important that the brain of this new life form be able to decipher the past lives of our souls upon entering the body. This was the most difficult part of new-man's evolutionary process. Due to the genetic link to the brain of Earth's primates, new-man could not recall the past life of the soul. Understanding our past lives is key in order to maintain a peaceful society and bring forth our technology in a positive manner."

"What happened while you waited for the Earth to be reseeded?"

"During the heating and cooling process of Earth, we continued with our experiments, including artificial insemination and gene splicing. We perfected in vitro fertilization. Eggs from the most physically fit and advanced females species from your world, and their most promising offspring, were frozen. At the appropriate time, those eggs would be thawed and combined with 'my' seeds to ensure the greatest strides in this evolutionary process. During those years, we visited neighboring solar systems. All were devoid of any species capable of crossbreeding. However, we did discover several planets that could potentially house our experiments.

Moreover, at that time, the Elders decided that the cargo we held was too valuable to take a chance by placing them outside their natural environment. At risk was the more than twenty thousand years of new-man's evolution. The need to create a life form, a shell, was detrimental to our existence.

Once the transformation of Earth into several continents was completed, it was time to re-seed the planet. All plant life necessary to preserve ecology was cultivated on each continent. After this transformation was complete, it was time to transport all physical and human life forms back to the surface. Each race of new-man was placed in different locations on the various continents with the intent of keeping them separate. The first born of each of those species were of my seeds."

When Daniel comments, "All God's children," the alien ignores it.

"Due to our intervention, the evolutionary process of new-man was phenomenal. We had succeeded in compressing millions of years of evolution into just a few thousand. Once the colonies of new-man were firmly in place, we began a recovery mission to return and retrieve the souls from our past world."

"But how?" Daniel asks. "You said that the energy force of the soul is too great to board your ships without a shell, and you are limited to the amount you can house in crystal."

"Yes, that is true. But the first generation of new-man provided the necessary shells. Once Earth's man evolved to meet our physical specifications, the first-born from each new species was brought aboard our ships and preserved. They were the chosen ones to house the souls from our worlds. Having gathered an ample number of shells, five of our six remaining cities returned to our past world to gather as many lost souls as possible. My ship stayed behind to watch over and further the enhancement of new-man."

Daniel argues with the alien. "You kidnapped us. You stole our very existence."

"We brought you forth. Without us, you would not exist."

A hint of anger is evident in Daniel's voice. "Maybe not as the humans we are, but most certainly as the primates we were. Each primate has a spirit. Isn't that what you said. Every living thing has a spirit and that spirit can manifest into a soul?"

"Daniel, we have given your world a gift."

"No, you formed shells to further your existence."

"Is that so wrong? Every day the people of Earth decide who lives or dies. We only create life."

"What about all of the living things you destroyed when you broke apart Pangea to form the new continents? And what about the physical beings from your past civilization? Did you not initiate their demise?"

The alien pauses and touches his forehead, as if he has become dizzy trying to defend himself.

"The analysis of the living beings on Earth was out of necessity. Furthermore, the demise of our people was not intentional. We do not sacrifice one life for another, as does your world. Violence was not, is not, a part of our existence. The violence of your world is a genetic flaw from breeding with the primates of Earth."

The alien's voice wavers. *"My son, I am weak. I must rest."*

Daniel lies quietly on the couch, eyes still closed.

Sensing the conversation is over, Mary interrupts his deep trance. "Daniel, can you hear me?"

"Yes."

"Ask God what happened to the souls left behind on Mars."

Dr. Martin inquires, "Agent Drake, what are you doing?"

Mary pays no attention to him. "Daniel, did you hear me?"

"Yes."

The Doctor tries to stop Mary's questioning. "I'm not sure that deliberately disrupting the natural process of his regression is in our best interest."

Again, Mary ignores him and tries to get Daniel to respond.

She repeats the question. "Daniel, ask God what happened to the souls left behind on Mars."

"I can't."

"Why not?"

"Because, he isn't here. He is resting."

Mary tries to prod him further. "Daniel, I thought that you were talking with God?"

"Yes, but I told you, he has stopped to rest."

Momentary silence falls in the room as Mary glances over at Dr. Martin, then back to Daniel.

Unexpectedly, Daniel opens his eyes and stares at the ceiling, hands fixed by his side. Uncertain what he is doing, Mary moves closer to him. Without provocation, Daniel grabs her face with his hands and forces her to stare into his eyes. While Mary frantically tries to fight him off, Dr. Martin hurries behind the sofa in an attempt to pry Daniel's hands from Mary's face.

With his firm grip, Daniel calmly states, "You know who I am."

The wind blows furiously outside as the aura surrounding his body grows more intense. The lights begin to flicker on-and-off.

Mary screams hysterically, "Daniel, what are you doing? Please, let go of me!"

Dr. Martin is unable to pry Daniel's hands from her face. The doctor huffs and puffs, and grows dizzy from his erratic breathing.

Daniel says nothing as he stares into Mary's eyes. She tries to look away, but can't. He draws her face to within an inch of his.

Mary desperately tries to look away as she struggles to free herself. Forced to look into his eyes, she becomes immersed in his soul, and visualizes several of Daniel's past lives.

Terrified by what she sees, Mary screams again, "Daniel! Daniel, please! Please, let go of me!"

Dr. Martin panics because he cannot help Mary in her struggle, and begins to yell over the howling wind blowing outside. "You've got to bring him out of it!"

Confused and frightened, Mary screams, "I can't!"

Hollering over the howling wind and furious clattering of things hitting against the building outside, Dr. Martin becomes insistent, "Mary, focus! Bring him out! He is still in a hypnotic state."

While the images of Daniel's past lives project themselves into her eyes, Mary is unable to focus and knows she has lost control. "I can't! I can't!"

"Drake, listen to me! You have to bring him out of it. Now!"

On the verge of tears, and with vision after vision churning into her mind, Mary makes an effort to break his trance. "Daniel, can you hear me?"

He does not acknowledge her. The glow surrounding his body intensifies, and Mary weeps in frustration.

"Keep trying!" Dr. Martin yells.

Giving it everything, Mary musters strength and cries out, "Daniel, listen. Can you hear me?"

There is no response.

She calms down and says, "When I count to three, you will awaken. One, two, three."

Daniel's eyes remain open as he wakes from his trance. His arms drop to the sofa. The wind outside grows still, and the aura surrounding his body disappears.

In tears and shaking uncontrollably, Mary falls back against the foot of the sofa in exhaustion as a river of tears streams down her face.

Bewildered, Dr. Martin stands motionless behind the sofa above Daniel's head.

Disoriented, and unaware of what just transpired, Daniel looks up to see Dr. Martin hovering above him. He briefly catches a glimpse of Mary running out of the room.

Confused, Daniel asks, "Where is she going?"

CHAPTER 7
Unanswered Questions

MAY 23rd - 1:00 p.m.

Distraught and hollow-eyed, Mary staggers into her office and takes a seat at her desk. Dr. Martin and Chief Rankin follow her inside.

Mary points to the two chairs on the other side of the desk. "Please, have a seat."

She interlocks her fingers and rests her hands on the desktop. "All right, gentlemen, you called this meeting."

Chief Rankin offers, "If it's okay, I'll speak first, Dr. Martin?"

Dr. Martin nods.

The chief rubs his cheek. "Let me explain the reason for this meeting. Earlier today, I received a report from the Area 52 lab."

"And?"

"Well, it is conclusive. The thing removed from Agent Scudder's nose is similar to those submitted for analysis from past so-called abductees."

"So, now you finally believe that Daniel might have been abducted?"

"No, I don't. What I do believe is that perhaps Agent Scudder implanted the ... whatever it is ... in his nose himself."

"What?" Mary glares at him. "You've got to be kidding me?"

Matter-of-factly, the Chief replies, "No, I am not. According to the scientist who examined the presumed implants, Scudder may have stolen one of the specimens."

"Oh, come on, Chief, I know that you don't buy that for a second."

"According to Tommy, the lab scientist, Agent Scudder brought him the latest sample to examine."

"He did." Mary confirms Chief Rankin's statement. "Daniel told me himself he was going by the lab on Monday, before taking the air-shuttle home. That was the same night he lost his memory."

"Yes, and shortly after Agent Scudder left the lab, Tommy began putting things away for the night. During that time he noticed a vial containing one of the specimens was missing. Tommy decided not to report the presumed theft until he had a chance to discuss it with Agent Scudder. He figured if Scudder did take the vial, he must have had a good reason."

Mary can't believe her ears. "Chief, Agent Scudder was there to drop off a specimen, not steal one."

"Phone records indicate that Tommy did place a call to Agent Scudder on the day of his disappearance. Tommy claims that when Scudder didn't answer, he left a message on his voicemail."

"Come on, Chief, I cannot believe that you bought that."

"Why would Tommy lie? He has nothing to gain from it."

Mary disagrees. "For one thing, Tommy would have jeopardized his own career with the agency by not reporting the theft. In addition, Scudder knows that, once submitted to the lab, those specimens become highly classified, top-secret evidence, belonging to the U.S. government. Why would he have even turned the specimen in for analysis if he wanted to keep it? After all, it was Scudder's idea to have the implant removed from each of the reported abductees."

Chief Rankin refutes Mary's reasoning. "It is my opinion Tommy was trying to protect a fellow agent. Given Scudder's, uh, mental challenges, we all agree Scudder will do anything to prove the existence of extraterrestrials."

"Where did you read that?" Mary glances at Dr. Martin. "In one of his reports, I presume."

Doctor Martin joins the conversation. "My dear, you can't dispute the behavior of Agent Scudder during yesterday's session. I showed the tape to the chief."

Mary is disgusted. "And your point is?"

The chief looks at her directly, "Drake, you know that Scudder is a very disturbed man."

"No, I don't know that at all."

"My dear, let's look at this rationally." Dr. Martin leans forward.

"Rationally? Excuse me, but I seem to be confused. We are currently here in the middle of a top secret facility which is building small-scale spacecraft in an effort to prove extraterrestrials might exist."

Chief Rankin responds, "Technically, we are here to advance our own flight technology for military purposes."

"I wouldn't know. Apparently, everything on this base is top secret. Neither Scudder nor I have clearance to anything here, except this building and the science facility at Area 52." Mary points toward the outside. "I'm starting to wonder exactly what it is the government is hiding out there in those hangers."

She opens a briefcase and retrieves several folders, then tosses them on the desk in front of Dr. Martin.

"Here, take a look." Mary is beyond exasperated. "I printed these out last night. They present the plausibility of Daniel's story under hypnosis. Go ahead; read them, it's all there. For example, Daniel Amen's study of the human brain, about the human flaw that allows man to kill, and Northrup's studies about The Death of the Dinosaurs and Volcanism." She thumbs through several more papers. "Here are various studies on the Blombos Cave project. Let me ask you something. Did you ever wonder how Philo Farnsworth, a Mormon farm boy, fourteen years old at the time, came up with the idea for the television while plowing a field or how Mozart published his first musical piece at the age of five."

"Then there's Hamilton, who mastered Latin, Greek, and Hebrew at five years old. Lest we forget, Theodore Kaczynski, known by most as the Unabomber, started out as a child prodigy, receiving his acceptance to Harvard University at the age of sixteen. Though not placing him in that same category, we should not discount our own Agent Scudder, the human encyclopedia, who you recruited because of his intelligence and fascination with the possibility of UFOs."

Mary continues her rant as she points to each folder. "And how about prodigies with brain disorders like Kim Peek, Alonzo Clemons, or Stephen Wiltshire, known as the Human Camera? Where did their knowledge come from? And how do you explain William Shockley, the inventor of the transistor?"

Dr. Martin interrupts her. "I'm confused about the point you are trying to make. What about William Shockley? He was a respected and renowned scientist in his field, and to my knowledge, he had no abnormalities."

"Yes, but why did he use his scientific platform to preach white supremacy? Why would this brilliant man jeopardize his career with such a racist notion? Where did that come from?"

"To what are you alluding?" Dr. Martin asks.

"I'm referring to the suppressed intelligence of the subconscious mind, and the alien's need to create the perfect race."

Dr. Martin and Chief Rankin look at each other a little confused as Mary continues to expound, pulling out the Bible and holding it up as she speaks.

"How do you explain the correlation between Daniel's quotes from the Bible and what God, the alien, told him? Daniel didn't just pick those quotes out of thin air. Care to see?" Mary sets the Bible down in front of them. "Gentlemen, for the first time in human history, this book is beginning to make scientific sense."

She pulls out more papers and photographs, placing them in front of her boss. "Here, Chief, take a gander at this."

Confused, but willing to go along, Dr. Martin and Chief Rankin glance at the pictures.

Mary shuffles the pictures around and begins to point them out with her finger. "That photo is of Wilhelm Reich. Are you familiar with his work?"

Dr. Martin answers, "Yes, as a matter of fact, I am. Before Reich lost his mind, he was hailed as the heir apparent to Sigmund Freud."

"Are you sure he lost his mind? He was much more than Freud's heir apparent. In the 1930s, his studies of biogenesis, the origin of life, were thought by some to be worthy of a Nobel Prize. In the 1940s, he claimed to have discovered a new form of energy that pervaded all space and life, a new paradigm in physics. One in which energy, not

125

matter, is primary. This energy was used to aid in psychoanalysis as well as heal physical ailments, such as cancer, with a device called an Orgone Energy Accumulator."

Chief Rankin replies, "Drake, I am also familiar with Wilhelm Reich and his involvement with the U.S. Government. But what does this have to do with Scudder?"

Mary becomes animated. "This energy reached far beyond physical and psychological uses. Reich designed the Cloudbuster Machine that modified weather, using the same energy. This was documented by a team of scientists and the media out in the Arizona desert."

He interrupts her. "I still don't ..."

"Please, Chief, let me finish. In the late 1940s, Reich discovered that the use of his Cloudbuster Machine attracted unusual lights in the sky. He later wrote that he believed these strange encounters to be extraterrestrial in origin."

"During this period, a freelance journalist wrote an article on Reich leading to his demise when Reich supposedly shot a UFO from the sky while experimenting with his invention in the Arizona desert, just outside of Tucson."

"And from everything you've mentioned so far, I can see why," the chief says.

Mary ignores his remark. "That article prompted an investigation of Reich by the FDA. Over a ten-year period, the FDA spent close to six percent of its entire budget to get this man who was unheard of before or since. The reason? Because Reich's work, his discovery, single-handedly threatened the use of fossil fuels. His life energy threatened the use of synthetic pharmaceuticals. Reich's discovery struck at the heart of the most powerful economic institutions and societies in the world. Billions, perhaps trillions of dollars were at stake.

"Add to all of that, his connection following the Roswell incident with the covert government activities involving extraterrestrials, and you have a dangerous threat to the rich and powerful of this country. The very people who controlled our government, and still do." Mary hesitates to gather her thoughts.

"Are you finished?"

"Not quite, Chief. When Daniel grabbed me yesterday and forced me to look into his eyes, I saw into his soul. Several images of his past lives manifested themselves in my mind. Most I did not recognize."

Rankin nods, "I read your report."

"That was until last night. I did some research when I got home. Those images kept playing over-and-over again in my mind. One in particular stood out. I asked myself who that person might be. And then, it finally came to me." Mary points to the photo, again. "One of those images was this man, Wilhelm Reich."

Dr. Martin chimes in. "My dear, how can you be sure?"

"Oh, I'm quite sure. Believe me, I will never forget yesterday's incident. I remembered a study I did on UFOs for one of my psych classes in college. I was curious as to what makes the mind create this phenomenon. That was the first time I had ever seen a photo of Wilhelm Reich. Then, I recalled a past conversation with Daniel and his fascination with Reich. He had a book written by Reich on his coffee table, and when I turned it over, Reich's photo was on the back cover. I know what the man looked like."

The doctor scratches the back of his head. "I find it difficult to believe what I am hearing. Drake, listen to yourself."

Mary picks up one of the articles about Reich from her desk and begins to read. "Listen to this. Keep in mind that Reich had nothing to lose. Reich was being prosecuted in a court of law, and his life's work had been taunted as absurd."

She alludes to the possibility that the government conspired to cover up Reich's work. "Supposedly, the FDA had destroyed most of his literature before the appeals process was even completed. With the work destroyed, Reich knew his reputation in the scientific community was finished, so he began work on his last article, *Contact with Space*. These are his words. 'On March 20th, 1956, at 10 p.m., a thought of a very remote possibility entered my mind, which I fear will never leave me again: Am I a spaceman?'"

Dr. Martin makes a face and turns toward Rankin. "This is ridiculous."

Mary looks at the doctor with contempt. "Dr. Martin, if you don't mind, please do not interrupt me."

Both men sit in silence as she continues to quote Reich.

"'Do I belong to a new race on Earth, bred by men from outer space in embraces with Earth women? Are my children off-spring of the first interplanetary race?'"

Having heard enough, the chief tries to end the discussion.

"Drake, I follow where you are going with this, but we need to resolve our purpose for being here."

Mary refuses to let it go and proceeds in spite of Chief Rankin's objection.

"Wilhelm Reich was imprisoned on a trumped-up charge by our government in 1957. If he was such a threat to society, why didn't the FBI, or the CIA, get involved? Why just the FDA? On the other hand, maybe they did. Reportedly, Reich suddenly died of a heart attack in his cell at the Lewisburg Federal Penitentiary, in Pennsylvania, on November 3rd of that year. Interestingly enough, Daniel Scudder was born eight years later in Reich's hometown of Rangeley, Maine, on March 24th, the same birthdate as Reich. Reich's institute still stands in Maine today."

Dr. Martin sneers, "Your proposal is absurd. Are you suggesting that Agent Scudder is a reincarnation of Wilhelm Reich?"

Mary answers definitively, "All I'm saying is, that without a doubt, I saw the image of Wilhelm Reich through the eyes of Daniel Scudder. Read into it what you will."

The doctor argues his own case. "There is no significance to having the same birthdate, even if it was possible Daniel is a reincarnation of Wilhelm Reich. My dear, think about how Scudder could be using his own knowledge of Reich and weaving it into this fantasy of the subconscious mind."

"I don't believe that." Mary counters. "I know what I saw. Nonetheless, there is more. I am agnostic in my beliefs, but as I recall from my theology class, and I looked it up."

Dr. Martin interrupts her again. "Of course you did."

This time Mary simply ignores him. "After our session yesterday, I remembered a passage from Exodus 13:21."

Mary picks up the Bible, turns to that passage, and reads. "And the Lord went before them by day in a pillar of a cloud, to lead them the way; and by night in a pillar of fire, to give them light; to go by day and night."

Dr. Martins asks, "Are you serious? You are comparing the cloud that Reich shot at, to a quote from the Bible?"

Mary looks at him, disconcerted. "Exodus 19:9 ~ 'And the Lord said unto Moses, Lo, I come unto thee in a thick cloud, that the people may hear when I speak with thee, and believe thee forever. And Moses told the words of the people unto the Lord.' God continued to speak with the masses from the clouds in order to frighten them into submission so that they would obey the laws that Moses would eventually present before them, The Ten Commandments."

Amused by her analysis, Dr. Martin grins and shakes his head. "But, my dear ..."

Furious, Mary has had her fill of Dr. Martin's condescending attitude. "Stop calling me that. I am *not* your dear! And as far as Daniel is concerned, this is over. No more sessions."

Chief Rankin steps in to take charge. "I'm afraid that is not possible."

"Well, then," Mary says, "have Dr. Martin probe Scudder. I'm off the case."

"I'm afraid I cannot allow that, either," he replies.

"Let me put it another way. I resign."

Stunned, the men face each other in silence.

Mary opens her desk drawers and removes a number of files. "As of this moment, I no longer work for the FBI."

Chief Rankin stands to confront her.

"Drake, you can't just decide in an instant you are leaving the bureau. Besides, at this point, you know Scudder probably won't respond to anyone other than you."

"Oh, well," Mary continues to place the miscellany from her desk into a box she obtains from the corner of her office. Her voice is filled with contempt as she addresses Dr. Martin. "I guess this effectively pulls the tent down on Dr. Martin's circus, doesn't it?"

"Be reasonable, Drake," the chief begs. "You can't resign. Think about your actions. Don't throw away a career, a lifetime of work, on the chance that your partner may be suffering from delusions?"

"Do you really believe, that Scudder is delusional?"

"Yes, I do," the chief says, emphatically.

"Well, I don't."

Distressed over the debate and the events of this past weekend, Mary is no longer able to control her emotions. She lays her head down on her desk and sobs.

Chief Rankin moves to where she is, and feeling somewhat uneasy about her state of mind, he makes a feeble attempt to comfort her. "Okay, Drake. Why don't you tell me what you think is going on?"

"I don't know, I don't know, I don't know anymore."

"I know how difficult this must be for you."

Mary slowly raises her head and wipes her eyes, then looks at him in disdain. "No, Chief, actually you don't. You didn't see what I saw yesterday when I was forced to stare into Scudder's eyes! You haven't personally been subjected to the events of this past week."

"True, but I have read your reports. I've seen the tapes from each of your sessions, and I've listened to your speech. I think that, maybe, we are all distraught over this entire ordeal."

"Distraught! Did you read my last report? I mean, really read my report? I saw over a dozen different versions of this man's past; as in past lives."

Dr. Martin cuts in. "My dear, it's not unusual ..."

Mary slams both hands on the desk in front of her. "If you call me 'my dear' one more time, I will slap you silly! I am Agent Drake to you! Do you understand me?"

Taken aback by her outburst, the doctor answers with care, "Yes. I'm sorry. I didn't mean to offend you."

"Well, you did. But that's another story. We'll deal with that later. For now, you will call me by the title that I have earned."

Chief Rankin leans forward and places one of his hands on top of one of Mary's. "There, feel better now?"

Mary pulls her hand out from under his. "I am not a child."

"I know, so stop acting like one, and act like the woman you are, an FBI agent for the United States Government, assigned to one of the most controversial, misunderstood, and exciting operations in the history of this agency. We need you to see this through. If we can determine what set

Agent Scudder off, we may well discover what this enigma we call extraterrestrials is all about."

Realizing the truth in Chief Rankin's statement, and how absurd her conclusions must have sounded, considering her own original skepticism about extraterrestrials, Mary calms down. "Okay, okay. I'll stay, and schedule another session for tomorrow."

"We can't wait," Rankin says. "Dr. Martin has already contacted Agent Scudder and asked him to come in today."

"So then, what choice do I have? None, right?"

Having smoothed the situation over, Chief Rankin is relieved. "See, I knew you would understand. I will be in my office while the two of you discuss how to handle today's session. Call if you need me."

Shifting his eyes toward Dr. Martin as he leans in toward Mary, he whispers, "Just for the record, I think he's a pain in the ass, but he's a damn good psychologist."

Dr. Martin cannot help but overhear, yet he dare not respond.

The chief walks toward the door. "All righty, I'm out of here."

He stops at the door and glances back. "Remember, we took on this assignment fourteen years ago in the best interests of our government, to put an end to all the hoopla surrounding the Roswell incident. We do not need mayhem in the streets over something non-existent. So let us get on with the business of doing our job, in the best interests of the people whom we were hired and trained to protect – in the name of The United States Government."

CHAPTER 8
Genesis

4:00 p.m.

Inside Mary's session room, Daniel has already been placed under hypnosis. The curtains to the room are drawn, and the lamp on the end table next to Mary has been turned on. Prior to Daniel's arrival, Mary emphatically informed Dr. Martin that he was not to interrupt her during the session. So, Dr. Martin sits quietly while Mary begins her line of questioning.

"Daniel, can you hear me?"

"Yes."

"Daniel, do you recall our last session? You were talking with the alien called God."

When he does not answer she refreshes his memory. "You were telling us how they came to Earth. How they brought their souls to this world. Do you remember?"

"Yes. God was telling me how they arrived here and why."

"That's right. Do you recall God told you he needed to rest?"

"Yes."

"Did he return from his rest?"

"Yes."

Daniel lies quietly, as if waiting for Mary to goad him for more information. "Did you question God further?"

"Yes."

All at once, a tempest begins to rage outside, and the familiar aura surrounds Daniel's body.

Though disturbed by this unexplained phenomena, Mary continues her questioning. "Daniel, tell me, what did you talk about when God came back from his rest?"

Daniel begins to speak in his alternate voices.

"I know you explained how you divided Pangea into several continents, but in the Bible, Genesis, chapter one, it tells how God created the Heavens and Earth in seven days. Where did this come from? What does that mean?"

"In order to colonize Earth, we had to prepare it to sustain life for each individual colony. We not only needed to keep each experiment separate, we also had to ensure new-man could survive. It took several attempts to create this new world. The seven days of creation is symbolic for each of those visits."

"I understand what you explained earlier, but I don't recall you telling me of seven trips."

"Perhaps it would be better if I explain in detail. Having studied your Earth already, upon the return of the six motherships to your solar system fifty-two thousand years ago,

we began the process of gathering all the species and seedlings necessary for sustaining life on your world. We continued the genetic manipulation between the primates of your world and our species on board our ships during this time.

From space, using the lasers onboard our ships, we divided Earth's one great continent into seven. This set off a chain reaction of volcanic activity on the Earth's surface. As lava flowed from the Earth's crust, new islands began to form beneath the great body of water. The ash that spewed into the air created a cloak that surrounded Earth, completely blocking out the sun. The intense heat eliminated all life forms that remained, most importantly, the dinosaurs.

After the great heating of the planet's surface subsided, darkness ensued cooling the Earth into a solid mass of ice. During this process, we abandoned Earth to explore nearby galaxies. We returned several thousand years later to discover the shroud of soot and ash had settled. The sun had begun to melt the frozen surface. Unfortunately, mountains of ice still covered much of the Earth's still drifting continents. So, we abandoned Earth again, this time to allow its surface to melt naturally.

Upon our third visit, we discovered huge bodies of water had submerged many of the newly formed continents. We needed this land to implement our experiments. Therefore, using lasers, again from space, we cut paths along the natural curvatures of the submerged surfaces in order to allow the water to flow unimpeded away from the land.

This dredging process would not be without repercussions. Volcanoes again spewed forth from Earth, causing the planet to heat, freeze, and then go through the melting cycle once more."

"So, there were two universal floods. It's starting to make sense. The Archeozoic Period of Earth's evolution, as explained in Genesis 1:2-8 and Job 38:4-11. And as stated in Psalms 104:3-6 ~ Who maketh layeth the beams of his chambers in the waters, who maketh the clouds his chariot, who walketh upon wings of the wind, Who maketh his angels spirits, his ministers a flaming fire. Who laid the foundations of the Earth, that it should not be removed forever, Thou coveredst it with the deep as with a garment; the waters stood above the mountains."

"Upon our fourth visit, we discovered a renewed Earth. As the waters flowed into the oceans, new rivers and lakes had formed, in addition to those shaped by us. Earth was now a planet with many continents, abundant with fresh water sources to support life. Some vegetation had already begun to grow in sporadic locations. We are uncertain of how Earth had already started this rebirth process, but were delighted. The planet was ready for re-planting. It was time to sow the seeds and roots we had gathered from the first harvesting and leave them to flourish.

We explored more solar systems while waiting for Earth's transformation to take hold. When we returned, it was time to restore the multitudes of living organisms, including the primates, with the exception of those chosen for the great experiments. Once in place, we left for it to rejuvenate. Upon our sixth visit, we arrived with our greatest accomplishment, the first new species of man, created on board our ships."

Daniel interjects, "Genesis 1:28 ~ And God blessed them, and God said unto them, be fruitful, and multiply, and replenish the Earth."

"Now certain this new species could survive on its own we initiated similar colonies from the iterations of new-man. Each species was placed in a select and remote area of the seven continents."

Daniel quotes another passage from the Bible, "So the Lord scattered them abroad from thence upon the face of all the Earth. Genesis 11:8."

"Genetically, we had created a variety of species in order to determine which breed would eventually resemble past-man both physically and mentally. Having established each new colony, we left them to survive on their own. When we arrived for the seventh time, to our surprise, new-man had evolved physically much faster than anticipated.

Fifteen thousand years ago, a child was born that closely resembled our shells. The elders determined it was time for one of our souls to enter that of the newborn child. That child was named Adam. Fourteen years after Adam's birth, a female child was born with similar features to ours. Another soul was chosen to host that of the newborn female. We named her Eve.

We decided to place Adam and Eve in their own paradise, a place on Earth that would allow them to exist freely, without predators, and lush with life-sustaining fruits. This process was repeated as offspring from each of the colonies gave birth.

Within a few years, it became obvious new-man did not have the ability to recall their past lives as they grew older. This was true for each of the colonies. We associated this with the primitive brain of new-man. A flaw associated with the primates. We viewed this as a major setback. Without the ability to recall the knowledge of past-man's soul, we presumed new-man would not be able to advance these new civilizations as rapidly as we had hoped.

We could not physically stay to guide them due to the acceleration of the aging process upon entering the Earth's atmosphere, and we dared not take the chance of aging and dying before new-man's evolution was complete.

In addition, all females and males onboard our ships had lost the ability to breed at this juncture in our history. Thus, a new quandary emerged. Furthermore, only a few of my seeds remained in the cryogenic state, deemed necessary to continue the acceleration of the development of this new species of man. We began to fear that without a host body capable of recalling the past, new-man would not survive or develop to our advanced specifications.

Along with those already deceased, when our people died aboard our ships, their souls were dispersed among the various colonies. Having placed many of our souls among you, we departed again, leaving the new societies to develop on their own. We could only hope that as time passed, the souls from our species would somehow find a way to guide new-man's journey.

Upon our return five thousand years later, Earth's man was nearly complete. The new progeny from each of the experiments had multiplied greatly. Aside from the color variations and height, their resemblance to past-man was astounding. Mentally, the mind of new-man had developed phenomenally well, despite the inability to recall their past. With guidance from the scientist from our worlds, all the colonies excelled at building communication towers across the globe. New-man grasped our knowledge well, perhaps too well."

"And on the seventh day he rested."

"That is where the book strays. We have never found a time to rest, if we are to preserve our survival."

"Why do we have so many different languages on Earth?"

"We formulated a unique language for each of the colonies in order to hinder procreation, should the various colonies of this new world wander and meet."

"Go to, let us go down, and there confound their language, that they may not understand one another's speech. Genesis 11:7. Why so many religions? And why so many variations?"

"The variation of texts scribed by our Elders became the tools we used for guiding the different species of new-man. Each book contained a unique set of rules designed for that particular colony in order to maintain separation.

The leaders from our six motherships often compared writings or metaphors, and then altered the text as necessary; based on the need of each individual civilization."

"You used religion and language as a way to control man."

"In a manner of speaking, I suppose we have."

"You created God. You created prejudice."

"We did this out of necessity in order to maintain separation. This was the only way we could be sure of which species, or race of new-man would evolve to resemble our past selves. We needed new-man to procreate, to create new shells. Free love could not be allowed as it was in our world. We needed fresh shells for our souls."

"Your book of knowledge most certainly had a purpose. Deuteronomy 21:18-21 ~ If a man has a stubborn and rebellious son who will not obey the voice of his father or the voice of his mother, and who, when they have chastened him, will not heed them, then his father and his mother shall take hold of him and bring him out to the Elders of his city, to the gate of his city. And they shall say to the Elders of his city, This son of ours is stubborn and rebellious; he will not obey our voice; he is a glutton and a drunkard. Then all the men of his city shall stone him to death with stones.

And then there is Leviticus 20:13 ~ If a man also lie with mankind, as he lieth with a woman, both of them have committed an abomination: they shall surely be put to death; their blood shall be upon them. Deuteronomy 22:22 ~ If a man be found lying with a woman married to an husband, then they shall both of them die, both the man that lay with the woman, and the woman.

Lest we forget Deuteronomy 22:20-21 ~ But if this thing be true, and the tokens of virginity be not found for the damsel, then they shall bring out the damsel to the door of her father's house, and the men of her city shall stone her with stones that she die: because she hath wrought folly in Israel, to play the whore in her father's house: so shalt thou put evil away from among you.

In questioning virginity, a rebellious child, homosexuality, and adultery, I believe, today, you would have wiped out half of the Earth's population. Then where would you put your souls? You do understand these rules take lives. People die every day because of the code of ethics you scribed for new-man to live by, and the prejudices you invoked into the societies of this world."

"The words death and die are meant as a deterrent. They are used to persuade those who run amok to adhere to our rules; a guide for mankind. We never meant for those words to be taken literally. A soul from the past, of our world, would know that."

"But you have already established the majority of the souls of Earth's man are not of your world. Therefore, new-man would not necessarily understand the intent of the written word." Daniel pauses to think. "The essence of your world, who became leaders of ours, are responsible for many deaths.

Stop me if even one of the names that I mention was not a soul from your world: Adolf Hitler, a man responsible for the deaths of 12,000,000 people; Leopold II, he killed 8,000,000 people; Jozef Stalin, an estimated 7,000,000; Hideki Tojo, 5,000,000; Ismail Enver killed 1,200,000 Armenians, 350,000 Greek Pontian's, 480,000, Anatolian Greeks, and 500,000 Assyrians. Boy, he was busy. Need I go on?"

The alien tries to stop Daniel's diatribe. *"They were confused. Their brains could not ..."*

Daniel continues as if the alien had not spoken. "Yakubu Gowon, 1,000,000; Leonid Brezhnev, 900,000; Jean Kambanda, 800,000; Saddam Hussein, 600,000; Mullah Omar, 400,000. The list goes on and on to infinity. Think of the number of shells that your world lost due to the evil thinking of those leaders, and all because their convoluted minds directed them to create a better society."

"We have tried to intervene and correct our mistakes as we sporadically visit your world. Unfortunately, new-man's brain assimilates its own rules divergent from our word, from our books, and from our knowledge. New-man has learned to manipulate our written word to invoke their own meaning, their own interpretations. This is due in part because the soul progresses, even though it cannot remember its past life while inhabiting the shell of Earth's man. The soul learns from each rebirth. This further escalates the evolutionary process of new-man. Unfortunately, the subconscious mind can convolute the lessons of the past, sending mixed messages to the conscious brain.

There are times when a shell on Earth will die, and we will intervene. We will gather that soul to place it elsewhere within your society, where it may serve a greater purpose. Often, this is done to accelerate the scientific knowledge around the world, and to slow the destructive patterns that have presented themselves in the past two hundred years."

"Question? As I recall, you stated each life form has a spirit?"

"That is correct."

"And that the spirit may manifest into a soul?"

"This is true. That has happened many times throughout new-man's evolution."

"Then it is logical that the simple, uncomplicated life of a primate on Earth would have evolved without the interference of your species. Therefore, each primate has the capacity to establish a soul of its own. Or, perhaps, in a primitive manner, the primates of Earth already have a soul."

"My child, there is no such thing as my species anymore. We are as one. Every human's existence on your planet is a direct result of our procreation. You are all my children. In addition, we have already planted 144,000 of our souls among you. These are the souls from past reconnaissance to our world and of those that have died aboard our crafts."

"Do you communicate with these souls during your sporadic visits to Earth?"

"As needed."

"Needed for what?"

"To further the procreation process, and to try and eradicate hatred, destruction, and possible self-annihilation because of our genetic oversight. For those reasons, even though we sustain our lives in the essence of outer space, our observations, particularly within the last seventy years, has been fairly constant. Our intent is to enhance the mental awareness of our souls that walk among you. They need to have a greater understanding of who they are in order to insure our survival.

New-man has reached a point in evolution that almost mirrors our past. The number of chemicals introduced into your society is destroying the physical attributes of Earth's humankind. In addition, the planet is being depleted of its natural resources at an alarming rate. Pollution is destroying its atmosphere. But most disturbing of all is how the people in your world have used our scientific knowledge to create weapons of mass destruction."

"We are a mess, of that you can be certain. Are the other ships watching us as well?"

"No, my son, our five sister ships are currently on a second recovery mission to retrieve more souls from our worlds. We anticipate their return soon."

"How is that?"

"The last Galactic Alignment took place in December of 2012. This was the window calculated for their return, although there has been no confirmation they reached this solar system during that time."

"Are you not able to communicate with them?"

"Within the past century, no. Cosmic storms may have knocked out our communication satellites and the various towers placed throughout the galaxy."

"The Mayan prophecies allude to a time of the end of the word of God. But is that actually the heralding for the return of the five crafts from your world?"

"That is correct. Once our ships return, a new dawning for humankind will take place. A new sense of direction will be created. Now that new-man has evolved to resemble our likeness, we will continue to gather our past souls and place them more earnestly among you. Then, perhaps, as we scatter millions of our essence throughout your world, it will reach a point to where there will be no need to hide our presence."

"How do you keep up with your people, the souls from your race who live among us on Earth?"

"We use a special device to track each of the shells that either house our souls or are of scientific interest to us. Once implanted, we can monitor their existence from space. Just like the device we implanted into your nose. Moreover, when one of our own is present on Earth, we use a form of mind regression to help the soul remember. They are not always aware of our

presence in the conscious state, but subconsciously we are able to communicate with the past soul, the inner self. Let me show you."

Though the wind howls outside, it is perfectly still in the session room. Mary and Dr. Martin wait patiently for a response from Daniel.

After a few minutes of silence, Mary intrudes on his thoughts. "Daniel, what is happening?"

"We are communicating, telepathically."

"What is the God saying to you?"

"If you would like, I can help you to remember your past, the physical beings your soul has journeyed."

"I would like that."

Daniel grows silent.

After a time, Mary becomes impatient. "Daniel, what is he telling you?"

"Saint Francis of Assisi was just one of your many lives. You are but one of our great souls which co-exists with new-man."

"No!" Daniel exclaims in his own voice. "This cannot be!"

"Yes, Daniel, it is true, you are my son."

Daniel whimpers like a wounded puppy. Then, he becomes silent.

Mary is frightened. "What does he mean by, *you are my son*? Daniel, is God still there?"

"No, he is resting."

"Why does he need to rest?"

"He is frail. I think he is dying."

"How long will he need to rest?"

"The last time he slept for several hours."

"Daniel, what happens while God is resting? Where do you go? What do you do?"

"I rest as well, but only for a few minutes. Between my sessions with God, I am allowed to roam freely throughout the ship. Though, I am escorted by two of their beings. They are really very friendly."

"Can you tell me about the ship? How big it is? What does it look like?"

"It's huge. I'm talking at least four and a half or five miles in diameter."

Daniel becomes excited as he gives details related to the spacecraft.

"In the center of the mothership is a dome-covered city. The city extends above the first floor. This is where all of the residents on the craft live. There are twenty to twenty-five towers in the city. They range anywhere from ten to fifteen stories up from the main floor and center of the ship, and are covered by a great dome. Moving walkways connect all the towers. However, they are not like our escalators. They do not have mechanical parts. I feel as though I am floating on air, as I move from tower to tower."

Mary is enthralled. "What about the rest of the ship? What does it look like?"

"The ship itself is saucer-like in shape. There are at least twenty floors below the city. Internally, there is a core. Each floor is connected by a series of shafts. These shafts replace our elevators. Once again, there are no mechanics; some kind of human energy moves you.

On the perimeter of the craft, an outer ring is connected by corridors, like spokes on a wheel. The center of the craft supports the city above and tapers off to only four floors at the end of the outer ring.

The middle four floors in the core of the ship are used for harvesting crops. Unlike our fields on Earth, these crops are grown in a controlled environment. Artificial light takes the place of the sun. Everything is neatly arranged in rows on multiple shelves. There is no place for the water to evaporate, so the humidity is constant throughout the artificial fields. Pollination is achieved with the use of Nano-bots. Therefore, there are no harmful bacteria or pests. This makes for an ideal growing condition. The plants multiply so rapidly, you can almost see them grow.

All life forms aboard the ships are vegetarians, and each apartment boasts an array of miniature fruit trees in individual pots. These trees take the place of our traditional houseplants. Everything is recycled, including their fecal matter, which is used for fertilizer.

Several floors are used as science laboratories. The lower floor, underneath the craft, is used to build and house their hovercrafts and other devices necessary for space exploration."

Mary asks, "What are the remaining floors used for?"

"The hub of the eighth floor is encased in a thick, glass-like material. It is called the energy chamber. A portion of this chamber runs thru the center of the ship to the surface. I can view this chamber as I pass between the other sectors of the ship's core. The entire shell of the ship collects energy from rays of light in space. Tiny shafts direct this energy to the chamber.

There is a huge control room, or bridge, on the top floor towards its outer edge. The floor below is a holding chamber. Also on this floor, there is a meeting room for other life forms, such as myself.

The entire base of the ship is made up of crafts which can adhere to the outside. They are exploration ships. Each craft is a fraction of the size of the mothership, and all house small crafts used for individual exploration."

"Daniel," Mary asks, "what about the other floors? What are they used for?"

"From what I could tell, one floor is where the experiments are conducted. In addition, it has several other sections. One floor in particular maintains a chamber used for storing the crystals that house their souls. When one dies onboard a ship, they collect that soul and house it there until it can be prepared for a shell on Earth. It is a heavily encased room. I estimate the vault's door to be two feet thick. Even so, as you approach, there is a glow, an aura, all around the outer edges of it.

I did not have a chance to see it all before I was summoned back to speak with God."

Having grown tired, Mary decides to bring Daniel out of the trance.

Upon saying the word "three", the wind dies down, and the glowing disappears. Daniel is back and sits up. He rubs his eyes and tries to focus while Mary looks on with grave concern. A tear trickles down one of her cheeks. Although he has no recollection of what took place, Daniel knows that whatever he conveyed must have affected her.

He kisses the palm of Mary's hand. "It's okay, Mary. It'll be all right."

THE NEXT MORNING – around 4:00 a.m.

Daniel and Mary are asleep in her bed. Outside, a shadowy figure passes by the bedroom window. Restless, Mary tosses and turns, talking in her sleep. "No, don't! Daniel, stop them! Please, Daniel, make them stop!"

Startled, Daniel awakens, realizing she is dreaming.

"Mary, wake up. Wake up! You're having a bad dream."

Mary opens her eyes and begins to sob.

He takes her in his arms, gently strokes her hair, and rocks her back and forth. "It was a dream, baby. It was just a dream."

Daniel wipes the tears from her eyes and notices fresh blood streaming from her nose. He touches the blood with his finger and then rubs it between his finger and thumb. "And on the sixth day ..."

Mary stops crying having heard his quote and seeing the blood. A look of horror crosses her face.

As if in a different dimension, Daniel is unaware of what he said. He brushes her hair back from in front of her eyes with his fingers.

"Lie still Babe. Let me get you a tissue."

Stunned and shocked, she watches like a helpless baby as Daniel reaches for a tissue on the nightstand.

CHAPTER 9
Time Is Running Out

MAY 24th - 1:15 p.m.

Exhausted and nursing a nosebleed, Mary sits across the desk from Dr. Martin in his office. With little fight left in her, she realizes they have no choice but to work together. Therefore, the tension between them has subsided.

Dr. Martin initiates their conversation. "I would like to arrange a psychiatric evaluation for Daniel. I think he may be delusional and in need of medical intervention."

Defenseless, Mary agrees and pauses. "I don't know anymore. I thought I understood it all, but now I'm not sure. One part of me wants to believe Daniel is losing his mind, and then there's the part of me that buys everything he has been telling us."

In his caring and understanding manner, Dr. Martin sympathizes. "Drake, I know how emotional all of this has been for you. So, if at all possible, I would like to wrap this case up today, no matter how long the session may take."

"I would agree, Dr. Martin, but I'm afraid to keep Daniel under hypnosis for too long. I have already kept him in a trance far longer than any subject I interrogated in the past. It appears the more he is under, the more he becomes a part of whatever is manifesting deep within his mind."

"I understand your concern. However, let me point out, if he truly believes his hallucination happened all in one day, how much more could there be to what he is telling us?"

Mary agrees. "It's just that I fear what he will say, or do next, as opposed to how long he takes to tell it."

"Agent Drake, if I may suggest, I think it might be a good idea if you are there for the therapy Agent Scudder will surely need after this is all over."

Mary declares half-jokingly, "I think I'm the one who will need counseling afterward, regardless of whether this ever ends. Admittedly, I was always the Doubting Thomas. Now I question my own thoughts on the matter."

The doctor is worried about Mary's mindset. "Do you believe his delusion is more than just a manifestation of the subconscious, a justification of his life's work?"

"Honestly, I don't know what to believe anymore. I'm trying to muster the strength to make sense of it all. For example, how do you explain the sudden windstorm, or the aura that surrounds his body every time Daniel is placed under hypnosis,?

You and I both know the glow has nothing to do with his skin discoloration."

Realizing her emotions are beginning to stir, Dr. Martin ends their discussion. "I would like to suggest we discuss this further, after today's session."

Mary wipes her nose. "I agree."

4:20 p.m.

Mary has already placed Daniel under hypnosis and helped him to recall his last encounter with the alien. Meanwhile, the wind blows outside, and that familiar aura envelops Daniel as he slips deeper and deeper into his trance like state.

"Go on, Daniel, what else did you and God discuss?"

Daniel validates his earlier statements with the alien. "The present man of Earth is unable to recall his past lives in a conscious state."

"This is correct."

"And this is the same for those of us with souls from your world?"

"Yes. However, new-man has entered a new stage of evolution. Many of our souls who walk among you have begun to be aware of their former selves, and have learned to incorporate that knowledge into the future. It is hoped that by doing so they can calculate a better outcome for humankind."

"How so?"

"Prophets, such as Nostradamus and Edgar Casey, Arthur C. Clarke, and spiritualists like Madame Blavatsky, have predicted the future in an accurate depiction. Even

writers of fiction have successfully predicted scenarios, and told of visions based on past life experiences. Those experiences may have come from our past world, aboard our ships, or from their former lives on Earth, or all three. In other words, their subconscious drew from the past and factored that knowledge into the evolution of new-man.

In addition to calculating man's next move, based on a past life experience, a spiritualist possesses the ability to communicate with other souls. That is because they are more in tune with their spiritual being, and the energy of others.

There are times, during our visits, that we plant subliminal messages in the minds of those we need to manipulate world events. We do this to create fear, or to offer plausibility to what could happen if man does not change his ways."

"Fascinating. Another form of control."

"The greatest leaders and scientists of your world were, and are, being guided by the souls of our species. Unfortunately, in many cases, the information or knowledge of the soul, suppressed in the subconscious, may manifest itself in the form of terror. This is due to the innate evolution of primate man."

"I believe we discussed this in our last session."

"Yes, but I need to explain further for all to understand." The alien acknowledges the possibility that others will hear the words in Daniel's transcripts when the sessions are over. *"For example, when Hitler's soul descended to Earth, it was one of a great leader, a scientist. His soul was placed among one of the first colonies. It was instilled in him that he should maintain separation. His*

soul had reincarnated many times prior to his rebirth as Adolf Hitler.

Remember, the human brain of Earth's man does not allow a child to recall, in the conscious, his past life experiences. As Hitler, the child grew into a man, his past life experiences surfaced in the subconscious to guide him, telling him the experiment must go on. The human brain of Earth's man often distorts the stored knowledge of the soul."

"Are you suggesting Hitler did not realize he was killing innocent men, women, and children?"

"Hitler in the flesh, yes, but his subconscious was leading him to experiment. His mind was directing him to perfect new-man, to become the man of our prior race, the race which best resembled our species."

"The perfect race," Daniel scoffs. "Why didn't you stop him? If you have the ability to create life, alter life, why not *intervene?*"

"We involve ourselves in your lives whenever possible. Keep in mind, we are not always present in your world, as is the case with Hitler, at least not until it was too late. Unfortunately, the original experiment got out of hand several hundred years ago, and most recently, we nearly lost all control."

Daniel is perplexed. "How?"

"Specifically, in 1908, one of our hovercrafts malfunctioned as it entered the Earth's atmosphere. We knew if it hit the Earth's surface, it could manifest into a catastrophe similar to what happened on Mars, for at least a part of the Earth. As it approached the wooded area of Tunguska, Siberia, we deliberately exploded the craft five miles above ground in order to avoid as much devastation as *possible.*

It was obvious that unlike the events or sightings of the past, we could no longer hide our presence. This incident brought our reality to the forefront, for many who walk among you.

But it was the event that took place in a remote area of Alamogordo, New Mexico, during the pre-dawn hours on July 16, 1945, that forever changed the world. In the early morning darkness, the incredible destructive power of the atom bomb was unleashed.

Man had succeeded in creating the greatest weapon of mass destruction, so far. We became aware our technology was being applied in a way we had not intended. Uncertain as to what extent Earth's scientists had elevated that technology, we watched over the skies of New Mexico during this event. One of our surveillance crafts was damaged from the blast and crash-landed in a remote area of San Antonio, New Mexico. We were able to recover our astronauts but had to leave the damaged craft behind until we deemed it safe to gather the crippled ship and bring it home."

Daniel remembers the incident. "Two young boys stumbled across the remains of what they believe to have been an alien spacecraft. I get where you are heading with this."

The alien continues his story. *"It wasn't until the crash of one of our smaller crafts in 1947, outside of Roswell, New Mexico, with two people onboard, that our existence was confirmed. One of our astronauts survived the crash. Both were taken, along with the crashed spaceship, and placed in a hangar at Area 51 in the middle of the Nevada desert. There, the dead astronaut you call 'alien' was dissected, while the* surviving astronaut was poked, prodded, and tortured for information. The craft itself was taken apart, piece by piece, in an effort to learn more about our technology. Your government now knew for curtain we did exist.

During that period of history, we had brief communications with your world, that is, until the leaders of your government challenged us. At first, they feared us. However, as they learned more about our existence in space, those in your government began to threaten us. They learned we were a peaceful civilization and would do no harm to the men of Earth.

Having already accomplished much with the Manhattan Project, and now atomic energy, they threatened to blow us out of the sky if we refused to cooperate. They wanted our technology, or they would kill our remaining astronaut. It was at this time we realized how hostile some of the human beings of Earth could be—beings we had created.

We explained how there were thousands of our souls already among you. Nonetheless, those who control your government are not the souls of our world. They are among the opposing souls that have manifested from Earth. Therefore, they rejected who and what we are. Theirs became not only a mission to hide our existence, but to set out and find the souls among you who are of our world.

Some had already been revealed to them, like Albert Einstein and Wilhelm Reich. When they discover a human being with a soul from our world, they often use mind regression to acquire the scientific knowledge from our past lives in order to manifest new tools of mass destruction. Your leaders intend to use those tools against us, if necessary."

"Why don't you protect yourselves? How can you allow these aggressive and destructive beings to control you?"

"Understand, Daniel that I, my species, have evolved beyond the ability to harm or kill. The ability to kill is a genetic trait of Earth's man, a flaw in the genetic transformation from primate to man. Until recently, we were unsuccessful in altering that flaw. However, there is still hope, for with each rebirth new-man becomes more and more docile, even with the opposing souls.

Time is running out. Present day man has created a platform of mass destruction that threatens the very existence of life on Earth. It is this threat we have prepared for over the last two thousand years. For the first time in our history, unless we can find a way to alter their thinking, we may be forced to rectify the problems that have reared from the opposing souls of new-man."

"Are you speaking of Armageddon?"

"Yes. Unless we find a way to control those who oppose us, we have no choice but to begin the experiment all over with those among you who understand our plight."

"You could have used your laser technology to end wars, to eliminate the evil that exists before it got to this point."

"We are the creators of all technology known to man. Your humankind chose to use that technology for evil, not us. Remember we are not always present. We cannot always intervene. Besides, direct interference might have jeopardized the progression of new-man."

"Hasn't your failure to intervene at certain stages of our development created the same scenario?"

"Yes, I suppose it has."

"Isn't it ironic? The very humans you created and manipulated would annihilate you in an instant, if given the opportunity."

"That is disheartening. It has always been our intent to create new life, not destroy it."

"What do you mean? You destroyed an entire planet, and I don't mean Mars."

"I am not sure I understand."

"I'm talking about the Earth as it existed before you separated the one great continent, flooding my world and eliminating all life left upon its surface. How do you justify the death of all living things that existed on the planet during that time? Is that not killing? Is that not murdering? Perhaps the term Playing God has true meaning after all?"

"Daniel, my son, I know it is difficult to absorb all about which I speak, but it is important you comprehend we gave Earth new life. We created the perfect planet on which life could thrive."

Daniel remains calm. "As advanced as your species is, you still haven't learned the value of life, have you?"

"I'm afraid I do not fathom your question."

"With all that your species has been through, and with all you have put Earth's man through, you still don't get it, do you? It isn't what man looks like, or who we love, that matters, it's that we love. If man concerned himself not with beauty, but rather with adoration for life, your world, our world, could live in harmony without destruction of self, of life, or of planet.

The body is supposed to be a vessel designed to house the soul. But you have chosen to manipulate the body into what your species has determined to be perfection. You have decided what the physical attributes of the shell must possess. It has been your influence of how we think of each other that has led us to the plausibility of self-annihilation—the necessity to separate the masses though your teachings."

The alien tries to reason this out. *"You don't understand ..."*

Daniel interrupts him. "No, I do understand! I understand you destroyed an entire civilization in the name of vanity. Look at you, the physical you. Is this what we are to become? You are leading us down the same path as the people of your world. You are responsible for this, not us. Is not the soul all that matters? Is it not the soul what unites us? You helped to write the New Testament, the Talmud, the I Ching, The Qur'an, the Dhammapada, Buddhism, and many other great books of religion. Do they not teach harmony, understanding, compassion and respect for everyone, peace, nonviolence and forgiveness for each other?"

"Each colony was given a unique book to guide them, based on their needs."

"Initially, you have to admit those books were scribed as a way to separate us, to instill prejudice among the races."

"*The Elders of our world did pen the great books such as the Bible, but we did not scribe the final word. As time went on, each book was altered, sometimes for the good of humankind, and occasionally to provoke evil. For example the New Testament; my one and only true son on Earth, the blood of my blood, the seed of my seed, provoked this writing.*"

"Jesus?"

"*Yes, my son. Despite all my knowledge, all of my advanced years, it is your understanding of life, of the immortal soul, that is needed if we are to succeed. You have a far greater understanding than I do, of how to move forward in this new world. Often the soul grows in one direction. Although it retains knowledge, and flourishes with each passing life, it becomes difficult to see beyond the physical once the soul is encapsulated inside the shell. Perhaps my species of man has placed too much importance on the physical attributes of man.*

However, you have never strayed. Your compassion, your appreciation for life in this New World, has never faltered. It is you who created the last addition to the book of guidance. It is you who gave new-man hope. It is you who regards forgiveness and acceptance as a way of life. It is you who gave Earth's man the strength to endure and overcome."

Daniel is unaware of what the alien is alluding to. "I don't understand. I'm not following you."

"*Two thousand years ago, a woman called Mary was impregnated with the last of my seed. She would eventually give birth to a child. That woman possessed a soul from our world, my soulmate for all eternity. The soul chosen to inhabit her child would be the same brave soul of the one whose life was lost exploring Earth for the first time, the same soul that guided Adam. That soul had been my child in past generations in the worlds from which we came.*

Perhaps it was the experience of losing life in such a hostile way, or of being the first born of new-man, that gives you a better understanding of our existence, of what really matters. The world needs you, Daniel. I need you. The time has come. My shell is dying, and I need to be with those whom I know and trust. I need to be with the meek and understanding, someone who fully comprehends life on Earth, if we are to change man's ways."

"Are you asking me to give up my shell for you to inhabit?"

"Not exactly. I gave you your life on Earth. I only ask you to do the same for me so that we may be together again."

"But why do you need me? You possess the ability to procreate with any woman on Earth, if you choose.

"As I have stated, all of my seeds have already been sown upon the Earth. Therefore, it is from your seeds that I choose to form a new shell."

"Why not choose any newborn child that comes into being?"

"You are a familiar soul, someone who can guide me as I learn about my new life on Earth. You are not an opposing soul."

"Define an opposing soul."

"An opposing soul is one that was spawned on Earth, formed from the spirit of the various life forms without our genetic link."

"I understand how the spirit may manifest into a soul, but does that mean every soul born on Earth is considered opposing?"

"I will explain. We were not always present when a mother gave birth. Initially, only eleven thousand of our souls were placed among the new species of man during the first phase of each experiment. It was not until the first reconnaissance mission that more souls merged with new-man of Earth. Therefore, the spirits of your world often manifested into souls and attached themselves to the birth of a newborn child. Those souls are the manifestations of all of the living things of Earth."

"How are they opposing?"

"The soul is its own entity. But, not every birth is associated with a soul, if there is not a soul to inhabit that child. However, every living being has spirit, and that spirit can manifest into a soul as the child grows, based on its experience with other living matter. Even if a child does not possess one of our souls, it can develop a familiarity with each entity it encounters while in the physical form. Therefore, it may not fear us. This is why like-souls travel together. Many souls create a bond which will last for eternity. They will choose shells closely associated within their world.

Furthermore, offspring from the original colonies often journeyed away from their own settlements, either to explore or to create their own society. If a soul of our world was not among those who strayed, the newly emerging souls of that sector of new-man became unfamiliar with our entity. Due to our higher intelligence, a physical being which houses a soul of new-man often feels threatened when they encounter a physical being housing one of our souls for the first time. In the conscious mind, they may not even know why. It is a subconscious notion that we threaten their existence, a fear of the unknown or unfamiliar. It does not matter that physically we all carry a genetic link. The soul steers the human emotions. We realized the potential for this to become a problem, and have done our best to instill unity among those who fear us.

When your soul was placed upon the Earth as the savior, it was to sway those entities who feared us. Even though new-man might never meet your physical entity, by believing in your spiritual being, your everlasting presence, new-man could redeem himself by accepting the laws of God; both those of the past and the appendages of the future. We had hoped that by teaching a new philosophy, new-man from every society would become less violent and more forgiving of each other, and learn to accept all souls.

In many ways that intervention succeeded. However, there is much to be done to counteract the unruly patterns man continually creates. There is no doubt the tools we used to control new-man, religion, languages, and prejudice, in many ways, have become excuses for war and hatred.

Despite this fact, with each generation, Earth's humans are becoming more and more compassionate and tolerant, even under the threat of war and violence.

We are in a time when the mind of new-man appears to have developed a greater comprehension of the soul. The human brain is starting to reveal more clearly the lessons of the past. You carry the genetic link that surpasses the ability to kill or harm others needlessly. You possess the ability to see beyond the physical. You are the last hope for the legacy of all mankind, for all that remains of this species both past and present."

"With all your species has gone through, why do

you continue this quest? What do you hope to gain from it? What is the purpose of life?"

The alien touches his forehead, indicating that he is tired and weak. *"Why do we carry on with this journey? There have been so many obstacles to overcome. Is it simply to procreate, to provide a shell for the soul, or could the soul live on without the flesh? I cannot answer that with complete certainty. Perhaps we do put too much emphasis on the human body. But, more importantly, is there something greater to our existence?"*

"And the answer is?"

"Only the Creator of all energy, of all things, holds the truth. The soul may live on for eternity, and man may ponder that question for as long. Moreover, the reality is, if we do not seek an answer, if we do not find a way for man to live in peace and harmony with nature and each other, perhaps our souls are doomed to wander aimlessly forever, or perhaps dissipate without a shell. This is the loneliness we feel in the flesh, in our hearts, and we fear for the soul."

"Much like for the wandering souls of your worlds."

"Yes, you are right, I greatly fear for all of those left behind on our former worlds. Are we doing all we can to save our species? Will we be able to preserve the new species that we have created on Earth, and if so, will it be in time?"

The alien pauses for a moment, as if barely able to think. *"Come, my son. It is time for you to return."*

"But there is so much more I would like to ask you, like the meaning of Stonehenge, the symbolism and powers of the great pyramids, and where the Nephilim's a crossbreed of new-man? Also, who are the souls from your world who walk among us today? And the list goes on."

"In time, my son, I will be with you, and you will understand all. But for now, it is time to go."

The conversation has ended. Daniel lies in silence.

"Daniel?"

"Yes?"

"What did the alien mean when he said that it was time for you to return?"

"It is time for me to go."

"Where are you going?"

"To my car, before being sent back to Earth."

Mary realizes Daniel is finished. "I'm going to count to three. When I do, you will awaken. Do you understand?"

"Yes."

As Mary brings Daniel out of his trance, the wind settles, and the sky outside clears. The aura vanishes from around his body and Daniel opens his eyes.

Dr. Martin sits quietly in his chair and observes the interactions of both Mary and Daniel, now that the sessions have reached a finale.

"Is it over?" Daniel asks, as though he already knows.

Mary takes his hand in hers.

"Yes," she says, "I believe it is."

CHAPTER 10
Soon We Will Be Together Again

SIX MONTHS LATER – 9:30 p.m.
AREA 51 – CHIEF'S OFFICE

Dr. Martin and the chief sit in front of a television screen. A televised briefing in Nevada is about to take place at McCarran International Airport, regarding the voluntary exit of both Mary and Daniel from the FBI.

"What do you make of this?" Dr. Martin asks as they wait for the briefing to begin.

Chief Rankin shrugs his shoulders. "I don't think they will say much. After all, what is there to tell? We hold all the cards."

"How's that?"

"Well, first of all, we destroyed all of the videos."

"But the transcripts were released to the public."

"Doesn't matter. By the time we discredit them, it will look like they are nothing more than disgruntled employees seeking publicity. The 'cleaners' have already begun the process of making the transcripts appear fake, made up. And, with the videos destroyed, how will they prove otherwise? Trust me, they will end up looking like fools. The believers will hate them for creating a phony story of abduction, and the non-believers will hate that they did it for the all mighty dollar."

"Do we know for certain they made a movie or book deal?"

"They will, once their money runs out. And we have made sure that will happen, especially when they are unable to keep their jobs.

"What do you mean?"

"We have our ways."

Dr. Martin is realizing just how powerful the man sitting before him really is. "So their lives will be ruined."

"Completely. And we will continue to deceive the public as to the true nature of Area 51."

Their attention is drawn back to the television screen as Mary and Daniel approach the podium.

MCCARRAN INTERNATIONAL AIRPORT
LAS VEGAS, NEVADA

Mary and Daniel stand in front of dozens of microphones, preparing to address the press gathered inside the airport. Both appear to be at peace, content with their new life. Now six months pregnant, Mary is showing. Placing her hand on her stomach as she speaks, and her wedding ring glittering from the flash of cameras as the questioning begins.

A reporter asks, "It has been several months since you resigned from the Terrestrial Project of the FBI. How has the agency treated you since you left?"

"As you already know," she answers, "the agency did not take kindly to my conclusion that Daniel may well have been abducted. However, despite our exit, the FBI has been very kind to us. After our debriefing, our boss at the agency has not kept us from speaking out or talking with reporters about Daniel's experience."

A reporter from a rag magazine questions, "So, you do believe he was abducted?"

"I did not say that. I stated Daniel believes he was abducted. My assessment of the sessions was inconclusive."

Another reporter yells out, "Daniel, can you tell us what it was like during your abduction?"

"I don't remember a thing. I only know, as do you, what was disclosed to me after my final session of hypnosis."

The same reporter keeps his hand in the air. "So, you cannot say for certain you were abducted?"

"I can only state I do not have a conscious memory of what took place. However, as I am sure you have read from the transcripts leaked to the tabloids, it is obvious from the conclusion drawn, my experience is hard to refute."

A reporter from a local paper thrusts his microphone forward. "Who do you think leaked the transcripts?"

Mary takes this question. "To our knowledge, the FBI is still investigating. Moreover, I can assure you we had nothing to do with it."

A local news anchor pushes his way to the front. "Mr. Scudder, according to Dr. Martin, the psychologist who sat in on your sessions, your entire experience is one of delusion. Something you made up to account for your failure to prove extraterrestrials do indeed exist."

Daniel is curt. "Dr. Martin is a moron."

Mary gently squeezes Daniel's arm before speaking, trying to prevent him from further comments. "I cannot say I believe, or disbelieve, with 100 percent certainty they exist. However, I do think it is fair to reason if one has read all of the transcripts in their entirety, it would be difficult, as Daniel stated, for anyone to refute the fact he was abducted. No one has ever thoroughly explained the aura that surrounded his body, the redness that colored his skin, or the sudden wind storms that arose every time Daniel was placed under hypnosis."

The reporter yells out, "Don't forget about the tiger."

Mary laughs. "That's right, let's not forget the tiger."

Another reporter from a local news organization hollers, "So Daniel, do you really believe you spoke with an alien named God and that you are Jesus Christ?"

"As I stated, I do not recall what I said. The story unfolded under hypnosis."

Without hesitation, Mary interjects, "I can answer the last part of that question for you. I've known Daniel for nearly fifteen years, and I can assure you he is not Jesus Christ."

Everyone laughs.

AREA 52 LAB

Tommy is finishing a long day's work at his lab on the Area 52 compound. He places a few new specimens in a vault inside the building. Once closed, Tommy rotates the lock and makes sure the door is secure. After taking off his lab coat and hanging it on a wall hook, he picks up his keys from a counter, turns off the lights, sets the alarm, and exits the building. He climbs into his car and drives toward the Area 51 compound to catch the shuttle craft home.

In the interim, a cloaked alien hovercraft has entered the airspace over Area 52. The craft is undetected by radar and the manned guards placed throughout the outer perimeter of both the Area 51 and Area 52 compounds.

The spaceship quietly lands a few feet from the lab Tommy just left. A shadowy figure exits the craft, approaches the entrance and using a handheld device, pushes a button that emits a high-pitched sound. The soundwaves break the glass to all the security cameras in and outside the lab.

Waving the gadget in front of a panel beside the door, access is granted, and the being invades the lab. Once inside, the alien makes his way to the vault. He uses the device and effortlessly opens the door. Having gained entrance, he uses a different mechanism attached to his wrist which activates a sound causing all the specimens from within to float, in unison, thru the air, out the door, and into his craft.

After he has all that he came for, he takes an explosive device from his jacket pocket and places it in the center of the room. Using a laser beam, the alien sets fire to every corner of the lab.

Mission accomplished, the alien makes his way back to his craft. He secures the latch and straps in. Under the cloak of night, the craft disappears into the night sky. A few moments later, the facility explodes.

AIRPORT BRIEFING

Back at the airport, the press conference continues.

"So, Mary, when is the baby due?"

"Mid-February of next year."

A reporter from California asks, "So, was this an immaculate conception?"

With a devilish grin, Mary replies, "No, we had too much fun making this one."

Everyone laughs.

A local reporter interjects, "What will you two do now, since you have left the agency?

"Well, I intend to take it easy until the baby is born. I'll worry about a job later," Mary answers.

"And I have accepted a teaching position," replies Daniel.

"What level?" a well-known syndicated columnist asks.

"I will be teaching the mentally challenged at all grade levels."

"That's quite a change from your work at the agency, isn't it?"

Daniel looks at the columnist. "I had considered teaching prior to my acceptance with the bureau."

A television reporter is disinterested in Daniel's career. "Mary, is it a boy or a girl?"

"We don't know yet. We want to be surprised."

An insensitive columnist inquires, "What do you think the baby will look like?"

Daniel finds the question distasteful. "What kind of a question is that?"

The reporter rephrases his question. "What I mean is, do you think it will resemble you and Mary, or do you think it will look like an alien?"

Mary grabs Daniel's arm firmly to keep him from entering the crowd and attacking the reporter.

She manages to restrain Daniel. "Should the baby turn out to be anything abnormal, we'll be sure and let you know."

Another local reporter at the back of the pack calls out, "Promise?"

"Oh, you can count on that." Mary glances down at her watch. "I apologize, but we must go. We have a plane to catch. No more questions, please."

A flurry of cameras click as Mary and Daniel leave the podium. Mary shields her eyes with her hands while Daniel leads the way through the blinding flashes of lights. He pushes the crowd of spectators away with one hand and grabs Mary's arm with the other. Finally, they reach their gate.

Upon boarding the plane, they take their seats near the front. Daniel sits next to the window. He and Mary lean back and relax as the plane smoothly leaves the runway and ascends into the heavens.

Once the plane reaches its designated altitude of thirty thousand feet and levels off, Mary closes her eyes and nestles her head into the headrest. Something compels Daniel to turn toward the window. He notices a bright light rapidly approaching. Several passengers sitting next to the window on Daniel's side of the plane also see it. A huge spacecraft rapidly appears. The pilot notices the craft and contacts the tower.

At the airport control tower, an air-traffic controller sees the ball of light in the distance. He looks down at the radar panel and watches the screen. The object approaches and flies parallel to the plane. The controller informs his supervisor.

"Sir, it appears a UFO has entered the air space of flight 207."

The supervisor walks over to the radar screen and observes the huge blip.

He asks the controller, "Have you made contact with the plane?"

"I'm trying, sir," he answers, adjusting his headset, "but all I get is static."

Inside the plane, the passengers and the crew panic, while Mary and Daniel remain calm. Daniel closes his eyes and hears a familiar voice inside his head.

"We are here to make sure you and Mary will be safe. Soon, my son, very soon we will be together again."

The End ~ For Now

The Alien Transcripts

ACKNOWLEDGEMENTS

I would like to thank everyone involved with the revamping and editing of this book.

Paulette K. Kinnes – My editor.

Sue Montgomery for proofing and corrections.

Fellow author Stephen Murray for his review, proofing and making suggestions.

Gracie and Angel – Two little four legged friends that bring so much love and joy into my life.

And Barry Goldberg – Life would not be the same without him.

ABOUT THE AUTHOR

James Kelly is a radio talk show host and the producer of "Aspects of Writing", "Senior Aspects", and "The Common Thread." He has conducted over 200 author interviews from all around the world on the topic of writing and publishing. He self-published his first book, *The Emblem*, in 1995. James writes in several genres, including children's story, *The Purple Caterpillar,* and is the co-author of *Weird Combinations of Food Women Crave when Pregnant and more ... Written by Two Men.* He grew up in the mid-west - Missouri and Oklahoma. For twelve years he lived in Atlanta, Georgia, where he began his writing and publishing career. For the past 20 years, James has made Las Vegas, Nevada his home.

www.ingramcontent.com/pod-product-compliance
Lightning Source LLC
Chambersburg PA
CBHW070704280626
47159CB00022B/1921